Lofty's main problem was that he hated challenges. He wanted to succeed in life, but he would have liked to find a dead easy way of doing it – like inheriting a fortune, or discovering he had a built-in talent that would make him turn rich without having to break sweat.

'Everybody's got something special in him,' he sighed. 'Somethin' really unique that can set him up an' make him secure. Findin' it's the trouble.'

By the same author

The Outsider
The Dark Side of the Sun

EastEnders Novels

Home Fires Burning
Swings and Roundabouts
Good Intentions
The Flower of Albert Square
Blind Spots

HUGH MILLER

Hopes and Horizons

EastEnders – Book 6

By arrangement with the
British Broadcasting Corporation

GRAFTON BOOKS
A Division of the Collins Publishing Group

LONDON GLASGOW
TORONTO SYDNEY AUCKLAND

Grafton Books
A Division of the Collins Publishing Group
8 Grafton Street, London W1X 3LA

A Grafton Paperback Original 1986

EastEnders copyright © BBC 1985
This novel copyright © Hugh Miller, Julia Smith and
Tony Holland 1986

ISBN 0-586-06814-7

Printed and bound in Great Britain by
Collins, Glasgow

Set in Times

January

Lofty Holloway had viewed the start of 1984 with anxiety. His fears and forebodings had nothing to do with what George Orwell had written; it was *Old Moore's Almanack* that had put the wind up him. The annual collection of grumpy predictions had told Lofty this would be a year of turning points, all of them tricky. It would be a year when he would come up against hard challenges, and if he didn't meet them squarely, and tackle them, his whole future would take a steep turn towards the gutter.

'I'm not one of life's go-getters,' he told Ian Beale over a fried-egg sandwich in Ali's. 'But I don't get the feelin' I'm a loser, neither.'

Lofty's main problem was that he hated challenges. He wanted to succeed in life, but he would have liked to find a dead easy way of doing it – like inheriting a fortune, or discovering he had a built-in talent that would make him turn rich without having to break sweat.

'Everybody's got somethin' special in him,' he sighed. 'Somethin' really unique that can set him up an' make him secure. Findin' it's the trouble.'

Ian nodded. At 15 he was eight years younger than Lofty, but his relative self-confidence narrowed the gap considerably. 'What you've got to do is follow your instincts. That's what the careers geezer at school said. He told us you get a feelin' for what you'll be best at.'

'I've had that already. But I can't do what I feel I'm best at any more.' For three years Lofty had been a soldier. In 1982 he had been discharged when a military doctor discovered he had dormant asthma. 'I was only half-way through my motor mechanic's course when they got rid of me. I've no qualifications, Ian. Even time-served blokes have trouble findin' jobs – so what hope is there for me?'

For a moment Ian considered eating the remaining crust of his sandwich. It had gone limp and soggy. He let it drop on the plate. 'I'd like to get into caterin', meself. In fact I wouldn't mind trainin' to be a chef.'

'Yeah, well, you've got a bit of skill in that direction.' Lofty dug through his change to see if the budget would allow him a Coke. 'I can't boil water without burnin' it.'

'Maybe your best bet's to pull a rich bird an' marry her.'

They both grinned at that. Lofty's manner and general appearance ruled out relationships with any but the most tacky females. Even the ones who were after a free night out rarely considered Lofty. His haphazard dress, his unruly hair and the gaunt, bespectacled, distant expression he always wore tended to give him a negative air. Den, the landlord at *The Queen Victoria* where Lofty worked three nights a week, once said that when Lofty walked into the bar, people got the distinct feeling somebody had just gone out.

Ali's wife Sue came bustling among the tables,

gathering up plates. 'You two finished?' she asked. Her frown suggested they had upset her in some way.

'I'd like a Coke,' Lofty said.

'Well you can come to the counter an' get it.' She picked up the two plates and moved on to the next table.

'What's bitin' her?' Ian whispered.

Lofty shrugged. 'Somethin' to do with Ali again, I suppose.' It was nearly always something to do with Ali. Sue was bossy and aggressive towards her husband. She was also completely dependent on him, emotionally and financially. 'He lost a few quid on the horses yesterday. Then he got drunk in The Vic last night. I had to help him home.'

'Poor bugger,' Ian mumbled. 'If she's anythin' like my Mum is when Dad gets legless, Ali must be goin' through hell.'

Nick Cotton came in as Sue got back to the counter. The sight of him deepened her frown. Nick was a short, stocky man who walked with the swagger of someone much taller. He leaned on the counter and tried to defrost Sue with his smile. It didn't work. Sue was too annoyed to respond to any friendly approach, and Nick was so mean-faced from his dedication to life on the criminal fringe that his smile radiated no warmth at all.

'Have you seen Ali?' Sue asked.

'Not since yesterday.' Nick put a fifty pence piece on the counter. 'How about a cup of tea, a bun an' a kind word, eh?'

Sue slopped tea into the cup from a big aluminium teapot, dribbled in some milk and threw a bun on

7

to a plate. 'Forty pence,' she snapped, picking up the coin.

'What about the kind word?'

'Don't eat the bun.'

Nick waited for his change, then he joined Ian and Lofty at their table. Lofty watched Nick cautiously as he took a couple of slurps from his cup. He had a way of bringing trouble with him, even in casual encounters like this.

Nick put down the cup. 'Glad I ran into you, Lofty,' he said.

'Why's that?'

'Still lookin' for a job, aren't you?'

'Yeah.'

'I might have somethin' for you.'

'He's not that hard up,' Ian said, grinning.

Nick glared at him. 'Shut it, you.' He looked at Lofty again. 'Your drivin' licence in good order, is it?'

Lofty nodded owlishly.

'I've got this mate,' Nick said, lowering his voice confidentially. 'He needs somebody to do a bit of drivin' an' deliverin' for him, three times a week. It'd be cash in hand, no questions asked.'

'How much?' Lofty asked. He still looked uneasy.

'That would depend on how much you delivered – you'd get an hourly rate.'

Lofty was considering ways of turning down the offer when Ali came in from the street. Sue was at him before he'd closed the door.

'Where have you been?' she demanded, failing to keep her voice down.

'I told you I'd got a taxi job on this mornin'.' Ali

came to the counter, trying to look offended. He had told Sue nothing about a taxi job, because there hadn't been one. But he could usually rely on her dodgy memory to get him out of a spot. 'Heathrow Airport, remember? I had to wait for a bloke an' he was ages gettin' through customs.'

'I've been slavin' here on me own since I got back from the doctor's. You didn't even open up for me.'

'Aw come on, Sue.' Ali, a Cypriot, had the ideal features for looking wounded. 'Don't start goin' on at me when I've been out tryin' to earn a few bob.'

Sue turned away and rattled a bunch of knives into a plastic box. 'A bit of consideration now an' then wouldn't go amiss.' She turned to him again. 'Especially after the way you've been goin' on lately.' There was the sudden trace of tears in her eyes. 'You *know* I've not been feelin' well, an' after seein' Dr Legg, well . . .' She tailed off and blew her nose with a tissue.

'What'd he say?'

Sue sniffed loudly. 'What do you think?' Her voice sank to a harsh whisper. 'He told me I'm pregnant, just like I knew I was.'

Ali's face struggled into reverse, trying to brighten. 'That's great!'

'No it isn't.'

'But you've always been sayin' how much you want a baby,' Ali insisted. 'An' we'll qualify for a council flat now.'

Sue moved along the counter and began to stir the beans that were simmering on the hotplate. Ali followed her. 'So tell me – why isn't it great that you're pregnant?'

'It's too soon,' she hissed at him. 'We're tryin' to build this place up. It's a time when I should be workin' harder, not slowin' down.'

Ali squeezed her shoulder. 'I'll just have to put in an extra bit of effort then, won't I?'

She stopped stirring and glared at him. 'You? Don't make me laugh.'

He ignored the jibe. 'We can get out of my Dad's overcrowded house at last – think of *that*. You'll be able to bring up our baby in a place of our own . . .'

Now she was openly scowling at him. 'Yeah, that's it – *I'll* be able to bring the kid up, while you're neglectin' the business an' throwin' away our money on horses an' cards an' anythin' else you can waste it on.'

'Sue! That ain't fair!'

'Now then, now then . . .' Nick Cotton had appeared beside them, holding out his saucer and empty cup. 'Not havin' a tiff, are we?' He tried his smile on Sue again and got the same response as before. He looked at Ali. 'Nice to be popular, innit?'

'I wouldn't know.' Ali took the cup and refilled it. Sue went through to the back and rummaged for something in the fridge. 'Listen,' Ali whispered to Nick, beckoning him along the counter and giving him his tea. 'Do you know of any poker games in the district? Good ones I mean, an' soon.'

'I could ask around,' Nick said. 'Things a bit tight, are they?'

'You could say that, yeah. I've been out half the mornin' tryin' to drum up a game.' Poker was Ali's strongest enthusiasm, and in emergencies it was usually his most reliable source of quick money. 'Let us know if you hear of anythin'.'

Nick went back to the table as Lofty was getting up. 'You goin', then?'

'Yeah.' Lofty pushed back his chair. 'I'm helpin' Den with some crates.'

'I thought you was havin' a Coke,' Ian said. He still had half an hour to kill before he went back to school, but he didn't fancy spending the time on his own with Nick Cotton. 'I'll get it for you, if you're short.'

Lofty shook his head. 'I've gone off the idea.' He had decided the one way to get away from Nick's proposition was to walk out on him. 'I'll have to rush, I hadn't realized the time . . .'

Nick detained him with a hand on his wrist. 'What do you say, then? It's somethin' kosher I'm offerin' you – all you've got to do is take a van round the West End two, three times a week an' do a bit of unloadin' here an' there. I'm doin' you a favour.'

Lofty gazed vaguely around the room, as if he was observing the flight of a paper aeroplane. 'Well, I'm not sure . . .'

'Christ Lofty, you've got to learn to be a bit more decisive.'

Lofty nodded. 'I know. People tell me that.'

Nick released his grip. 'You're workin' in The Vic Friday night, right? Tell me then. My mate's got to get an answer before the weekend.'

Lofty reluctantly agreed to that. He hesitated as Ian got up to leave with him. 'Listen, Nick – this job, how come your mate's havin' trouble gettin' a

11

driver? I'd have thought there was plenty knockin' about.'

Nick's eyes became guarded. 'There's lots of good drivers about, yeah. But he's after somebody honest an' reliable. That kind's harder to come by.'

Lofty looked mildly flattered. 'Oh, I see. Well, I'll let you know on Friday, right?' He waved awkwardly and moved off with Ian behind him. As they passed the counter Ali was telling Sue she should learn to put more trust in him.

The dry-mouthed, let-down feeling that followed Christmas and the New Year celebrations was evenly spread around Albert Square. At No 43, the male nurse Andy O'Brien and his girlfriend, Debbie Wilkins, had embarked on a campaign of further house improvements to see them through the rest of the winter. Next door, Lou Beale put festive goodwill behind her and had reverted to her role of stern but even-handed matriarch. As part of her regime of letting no one get complacent about anything, she warned her son-in-law, Arthur Fowler, that he had to take serious heed of the rumblings about redundancy at the factory where he worked.

'Get out an' start lookin' for another job right now, instead of waitin' until you're on the dole.'

Arthur said he would do that. He said it to get peace. Things were hard enough with himself, his wife and two children living under the same roof as Lou, without taking on any extra pressure. In Arthur's opinion the redundancy rumours were hollow. There were still plenty of orders on the factory's books, and even if the management did start trimming the work-force he was safe. He had been there for sixteen years.

'It's last in, first out at our place,' he reassured his wife, Pauline. She took a large measure of comfort from what he had said; nevertheless, because she was a cautious and practical woman, she had already applied for part-time work at the launderette round the corner on Bridge Street.

At *The Queen Victoria*, on the corner opposite Lou Beale's house, the first days of January had passed with the customary New-Year hostility fizzing in the air. Den Watts and his wife Angie had never been able to get a grip on harmony, although they always showed their customers a bright, united front. This year, the main barriers to domestic peace were Den's continuing affair with an up-market lady called Jan, and Angie's return to the bottle after a long spell of abstinence. Each blamed the other for their weakness.

'Is it any wonder I drink?' Angie demanded. It was ten minutes before opening time on the evening of Friday, the 6th of January. Den had just come into the bar and found her sinking a large gin. From the look of her, it wasn't the first. 'What woman,' she wailed, 'could stay sane *and* sober with a husband who never touches her – a husband that saves all his lovin' for some trollop up West? A husband who – '

'Belt up, Ange,' Den warned her. 'The only reason I've got an arrangement elsewhere – an' not with no trollop, neither – is because my day-to-day life here's a bloody nightmare. An' why? Because my lady wife's a lush, that's why. An' when she's not bein' a lush she's off hawkin' her mutton somewhere.'

Angie stiffened. 'You lyin' bastard!'

'No, I'm not.' Den leaned forward, his forehead almost touching hers. 'Do you want me to shove proof under your nose? Do you?'

Angie didn't want to go that route. 'Piss off,' she snarled, reaching for another drink.

'Put down the glass an' get upstairs.'

Her eyebrows rose. 'My, my Denis, what *have* you got in mind? Beddy-byes, is it? A bit of a naughty?' Her voice and face hardened abruptly. 'Fat chance of that, isn't there?'

'Listen,' Den said, 'I want you to go up an' tidy yourself. Straighten your hair. Touch up the powder an' paint. I don't want the clientele seein' you lookin' like Old Mother Riley.'

She stood her ground stubbornly. 'They'll take me the way they find me, or they can lump it.'

Den grasped her by the shoulders. 'If you don't sort yourself out, girl, I'm bannin' you from this bar. Got that? If you want to get piss-witted every night, do it in some other pub.' He tightened his grip and shook her once, hard. 'Don't think I'm kiddin'. I mean it.'

Angie sagged suddenly, staring at him. 'All right,' she said in a small voice. 'Just let me go.' As he took away his hands she stepped back, still staring. 'Here's somethin' for *you* to get into your head while I'm upstairs puttin' on me veneer. If you can't lay lovin' hands on me, don't lay violent ones on me. Not ever. If you do it again, I'll leave you.'

14

Den couldn't resist a sneer. 'You tried that before, remember?'

Three years ago, Angie had walked out. She had come back within ten days, after discovering she couldn't live without Den.

'I'm harder now,' she said. 'Older. I wouldn't be back with me tail between me legs next time.'

Den watched her turn and make her way towards the stairs. He wouldn't say it, he thought, he wouldn't tell her to go ahead and leave. She might just do it. For reasons he was weary of going over, year in and year out, he simply couldn't manage his life without her. Which was a pity, he reflected bitterly. It was no great joy to be emotionally bound to a woman he could scarcely bring himself to like.

By seven-thirty the place was busy. Fridays and Saturdays had more pattern than other nights; Den, Angie and Lofty moved briskly about the two bars, predicting orders and making stock responses as history steadily repeated itself.

'This weather gets right into your bones,' Ethel Skinner said as Angie poured her a Guinness. Ethel was the pub's cleaner. She was also Albert Square's repository of gossip, its resident clairvoyant, a habitual matchmaker among the middle-aged and the most eccentrically dressed old lady for miles. 'I don't like givin' in to the effects of the cold, you know, but there's times I could despair for me knee joints.'

'Get that down you, Ethel,' Angie said, passing across the drink. 'It'll soon drive out the twinges.'

Every week in winter it was the same opening exchange; in spring it would be something about the days getting longer, then in summer it would be

15

either the terrible weather for the time of year, or the debilitating heat. But Angie didn't mind the repetitiveness of weekends. It put a small, necessary sense of order into her life. As she turned from serving Ethel she was confronted by another segment of the Friday pattern. Pete Beale and his wife Kathy were coming up to the bar. There was a difference tonight, though. Neither of them was smiling at her.

'Hello, kids. How's tricks?'

Pete looked at her balefully. Kathy, who was Angie's best friend, threw her a warning frown. Angie promptly toned down the brightness.

'The usual, is it?'

'Please,' Pete grunted.

Angie got the drinks, took the money and handed back the change. Then she stood where she was, even though other people were waiting to be served. 'Right,' she said. 'Tell me. I can't have all this gloom in here without knowin' why.'

Pete seemed reluctant to say anything. He looked at Kathy for a moment, then shrugged. 'It's a bit of a business worry we've got, love.'

Angie frowned. 'Trade bad, is it?' Seasonal dips in trade were hardly unusual. 'There's not a lot of money about at this time of year,' she pointed out. 'Things always start pickin' up in February an' March.'

'We've been takin' that into account,' Kathy said. 'But things have never been as bad as this. Unless we've a hell of a rush on the stock tomorrow, we reckon we'll be forty per cent down on this time last year.'

'Forty per cent?' It was Den who spoke. He came along the bar with a half-pulled pint in his hand. 'Bloody hell, mate, that's a bit serious.'

'You're tellin' me.' Pete lifted his drink and gazed at it. 'The reason's even more serious, though.'

Den nudged Angie. 'Here,' he said, handing her the half-full glass. 'Fill that up an' give it to Arthur Fowler, will you?' Annoyed, Angie snatched the glass and went off with it. Den leaned his elbows on the bar. 'So what's the reason?'

'Competition,' Pete said.

'What – on the market?' Pete's was the oldest fruit and vegetable stall operating in Walford. His mother, Lou, had worked on it with his father long before the war. 'I can't see anybody offerin' you much opposition out there.'

'It's not on the market,' Kathy said. 'It's a shop. They opened on Monday an' they're undercuttin' us somethin' horrendous.'

Den still looked unconvinced. 'With rent an' rates an' all the rest of it to cope with? How do they manage to undercut?'

Pete explained. The shop, only a few yards from the top end of the market, was part of a consortium. Pete still didn't know who they all were, but he did know they were buying fruit and vegetables in huge bulk and cutting prices to a level where he couldn't even make a profit.

'So what'll you do?'

Pete shrugged. 'We just wait an' see if the novelty wears off an' people get loyal again. Not much hope of it, though. Not at them prices.'

As Den was trying to think of something encouraging to say, Lofty was at the far end of the bar being lectured by Dr Legg. In addition to being the local GP, Legg was also the landlord of Lofty's one room flat in the square.

'There comes a time,' the doctor was saying, 'when excuses, even ingenious excuses, don't impress me. Believe it or not, my heart isn't all that hard, Lofty. It's my patience that's the problem. It's worn terribly thin with all your waffling and delay. It's threadbare, in fact.' He leaned across the bar and lowered one bushy eyebrow, then the other. 'I want the rent by tomorrow at the latest. It's been three weeks and I'm not prepared to wait any longer.'

Lofty opened his mouth to deliver another excuse, then decided he shouldn't. There was no sense in using them all up at a time when the doctor wasn't even going to listen.

'I'll have it for you,' he said, blinking behind his glasses. 'I've just had a bit of trouble lately . . .'

'Haven't we all, Lofty, haven't we all.'

As Dr Legg turned away with his glass of wine Nick Cotton sidled along the bar.

'Well?' he said. 'Got an answer for me, have you?'

Lofty looked at him, stumped for the moment. Then he remembered. 'Oh. Yeah. Well, I've sort of thought it over, but I've not had time to finally make up me mind . . .'

Nick set his teeth, looking as if he would like to hit Lofty.

'You have to think over a thing like this, don't you? I like to look at all the angles . . .'

'Bollocks!' Nick hissed. 'Look, there's nothing to think about. You're bein' offered good money to do somethin' easy. If you want to think about somethin', think about the jam you're gettin' in with him.' He jerked his thumb towards the corner where Dr Legg had sat down. 'I was listenin' just then. How much are you into him for? Forty-five quid, maybe? Where the hell are you goin' to get that kind of bread in a handful? The longer you tit about the more you'll owe him an' the harder it'll be to get dough together. You'll be out on your arse before you know it if you don't do somethin' fast.'

Lofty stood there confronting the sudden spectre of homelessness. For all he knew, the doctor might just throw him out, like Nick was saying. Then what? He would have to go back to his mother's place. God, he thought, nothing was worse than that. She nagged him worse than ten Dr Leggs ever could.

'Right,' he said, as decisively as he was able. 'I'll take you up on it.'

Nick brightened at once. 'No backin' down now, eh? I can tell me mate you're on, then he'll let me know when you can start. It's as simple as that.' He winked. 'When did you last get a job that easily?'

'Yeah. Right. Thanks a lot, Nick.' Lofty stared at his knuckles. What was he letting himself in for, he wondered. Nick Cotton was as bent as a paper clip. He *never* got involved with anything straight. 'You're sure it's all on the level? I'll just be drivin' an' deliverin'?'

'That's it.' Nick glanced towards the telephone. 'I'll speak to him now. You can pull me a pint an' pay for it, as a little bit of a thank-you.'

'Sure.' Looking very troubled, Lofty got a glass and took it to the pump.

At the telephone Nick dialled and waited. When the number was answered he pushed in the coin and cupped his hand to the mouthpiece.

'Hello, Barry? It's me, Nick. I've done it, like I said I would. I've found just the man for you.' He paused, nodding at the receiver. 'Don't worry, I got the specification dead right. Dumb but capable. No curiosity, does what he's told. Typical ex-army berk. He won't make no waves an' the best thing is he's clean, no form whatsoever, so he won't attract the Pigs' attention. Better still, he's got no mates to start gettin' interested in what he's doin'.' There was another pause, punctuated with nods. 'I wouldn't do nothing' to cut me own throat, would I? This lad's on the ball as a driver an' all the rest of it – but when it comes to savvy, he's as thick as shit in the neck of a bottle. Stand on me.'

A couple of seconds later he hung up and went back to the bar. His pint was waiting. He lifted it and made the gesture of a toast towards Lofty, who was serving a customer. 'Good health,' he murmured, and took a long, deep gulp.

On January 16th the Ford Motor Company announced that their Dagenham foundry would close within fifteen months, with a loss of two thousand jobs. Lou Beale believed the news was ominous: 'If a well established place like that can go,' she said, 'then no factory jobs are safe any more.'

Once again, Arthur Fowler found himself being grilled about his prospects of work elsewhere, if he should lose his job. He assured both his wife and his mother-in-law that he was still looking. He also assured them that the Ford closure was a separate issue – it was something that didn't affect the branch of industry he was in. Secretly, he began to wonder if this was an omen, just as Lou had said. There was no denying that factories seemed to be closing down all over the place. Without a job, he had no idea how he would cope; finding another one wouldn't be easy, either. Not for a man of forty-two living in a country where more than three million people were already out of work.

For Ali Osman there were economic problems, too, although their scale and nature were a lot different from the difficulties Arthur saw looming. On the same grey Saturday that Ford's made their closure announcement, a bookie called Doug Fleming made one of his own.

'The horn of plenty's shut on you, Ali my son. No more credit, an' I want the money you owe me within one week of today.'

Ali had seen it coming, but it was still a shock. He looked round the tiny office where Doug had summoned him. It was bleak and mean, the very mirror of its owner.

'I'm doin' this for your own good, son. You don't want to go gettin' in any deeper, do you?'

Ali held up the slip he had been filling in when

Doug sent for him. 'Can I put this one bet on? Just the one, Doug . . .'

'At my expense?' Doug smiled coldly, displaying yellow predator's teeth. 'Don't be daft. I only let you have credit in the first place because you've been a steady punter.'

'An' I'll go on usin' this place.'

The promise of continued patronage cut no ice with Doug. He squared his bulky shoulders and sighed. 'Ali, I never had you down for a loser. But it's what you are – or it's what you've turned into. I've seen it before. One losin' streak can do it. You catch fright, an' the next thing you know, you've lost your feel for the horses. You can't spot a winner in a two-nag race.'

'Nah, it's not like that with me . . .'

'Yes it is.' Doug tapped the side of his skull. 'Anxiety got in the way of your judgement. Before you knew it, you'd be bettin' like an old lady – pickin' names that sound right, numbers that look lucky, all that crap.' He shook his head slowly. 'No more tick, an' that's final.' He glanced sideways at the ledger on his desk. 'You owe me two hundred an' ninety notes. That's the bottom line, Ali. I want the lot, no later than twelve noon on the twenty-third.'

'Aw please Doug, let me have a chance to even up – I mean how else can I get the money?'

'I've heard you're pretty sharp at raisin' the read-ies when you have to.' Doug pulled open the door. 'Believe me, in this case you *have* to.' He stood aside to let Ali out. 'See you next Saturday, if not before.'

Out on the street Ali stood by the betting shop window, staring at the crudely painted horses with their gaudy, ill-proportioned jockeys, all passing the post at the same time. What the hell was he going to do?

It wasn't easy to take stock without panicking. There was the best part of three hundred due to Doug. A sure-fire poker game, five nights before, had turned into a disaster because he hadn't been concentrating; he had lost his cool and bluffed wildly on a pair of twos. The upshot was he now owed Den Watts the fifty quid he had borrowed for his stake. Then there was the rates money for the café, which he didn't have because it had gone on two horses. There was the Inland Revenue, who'd made what they called a retrospective assessment on him and now wanted two hundred and thirty pounds to square matters. There were the bills for café supplies, for electricity, gas, petrol. There were enough debts to send him out of his head with worry.

He turned and looked along the street. It was starting to rain. People were scurrying into shops and doorways. Ali thought of Doug again. It was more than worry he felt there. Given another hour of thinking about the bookie, he would be in the grip of shivering fear. There had been no need for Doug to outline what would happen if the money wasn't paid. Every betting man in Walford knew. A few of them carried the marks as proof.

Ali began to walk, his head tucked down against the rain. There had to be a way out. A few measly hundred quid would solve everything. He tried to hold that thought, he struggled to make it minimise his problem. But it was no good. A few measly hundred was a lot when all you had was an ultra-measly fourteen quid to your name.

"What am I gonna do?' he groaned against the stinging rain.

At times like this he wished he could do what his old mother had once told him; he wished he could believe that his problems were nothing, nothing at all when he imagined himself as no more than a speck of dust in a huge, endless universe. But he couldn't imagine himself as anything but a spotlit, vulnerable man carrying a whole galaxy of worries and dreads. It would have been nice to think what the hell, let it all happen, I don't care a damn, nothing can hurt me. Nice as it might be, Ali suspected nobody but a man with severe brain damage could feel like that.

A hand landed heavily on his shoulder with a slap. Ali froze, his heard thumping. He turned and saw Nick Cotton grinning at him.

'You look scared, mate. Who did you think I was? The Bill?'

'Do me a favour,' Ali rasped. 'Don't sneak up on me like that again.'

'All right, all right, keep your rug on.' Nick wiped the rain from his face and looked across the road. He pointed. 'Fancy a drink? The Tatlock's beer ain't much cop, but they've got nice barmaids.'

Ali shook his head. 'A drink's the last thing I want.' He started to move away. 'I've got to get back. Sue'll be havin' a fit.'

'OK,' Nick said. 'If you don't want to hear about a game, don't bother.'

Ali stopped. 'What game?'

'Buy us a pint an' I'll give you the details.'

The interior of the pub was bright and brassy, an Edwardian working men's saloon that had miraculously escaped the ravages of age and the developers. Men leaned in one long row at the oak-topped bar, some evaluating their reflections in the bronzed mirrors at the back, but most eyeing the barmaids as they half-listened to each others' aimless talk. Nick found a gap between two drinkers and edged Ali into it.

'I'll have a pint an' a scotch, mate.'

'You've got a right cheek,' Ali grunted. 'The information better be worth this.'

They took their drinks to a table and sat down. Nick swallowed the whisky in two gulps and washed it down with a mouthful of beer. He winked at Ali and leaned close. 'What would you say to a five-hander, stud, with four other blokes who're amateurs with more money than sense?'

'I'd say it's a grass dream,' Ali sighed. 'There's not many games like that nowadays. Poker's catchin' on. It's like snooker. There's a lot of bright guys where there used to be a load of wallies.'

'It's straight,' Nick insisted. 'I've checked. You asked me to, remember?'

Ali held up a hand. 'I didn't ask you to check around. Don't make out you've been doin' me some big favour, Nick. I said if you heard of anythin', let me know.' It was important never to let Nick make you believe he was a concerned ally, a pal who had done you a few good turns. That way lay quicksand.

He was prone to ask difficult favours that some people felt too obligated to refuse.

'Well, whatever. The blokes I'm on about are two oil-rig workers an' a couple of Pakis.'

Ali frowned. 'That doesn't sound like a very likely combo to me . . .'

Nick sat back sharply and folded his arms. 'If you don't believe me, just come out an' say so. Then I'll keep me trap shut.'

'Go ahead,' Ali sighed.

Nick took another gulp of beer and gave him the details. The oil men were on a two-month break in London. They had ventured into the East End one night and met up with the Pakistanis, who ran a late drinks club in Walford. After some talk, they discovered a mutual liking for games of chance, among them stud poker. They met and played twice and sometimes three times a week. From their talk, which Nick had carefully listened to in a pub, he had gathered they were prime chancers.

'Enthusiastic, you know? But all the time they were on about beatin' each other with shitty hands, as if that was the purpose of the game. You know the kind of prawns I'm on about. You've skinned a few of them in the past.'

Ali certainly had. But never four at a time. It sounded like a dream come true – which meant, with his recent luck, that he would probably walk into a hustlers' ambush. But he had to try something. So far this was all he had.

'How do I get in touch with them?'

'They meet in the Carver's Arms every Saturday. If you're goin' to get somethin' together with them

26

you'll have to move fast. The oil blokes are goin'
back up north on Tuesday.'

'Do they know you?'

Nick nodded. 'I've put them on to one or two
odds an' ends they were after.'

That could mean drugs or women, Ali thought,
or probably both. 'You'll introduce me then, will
you?'

'Sure,' Nick said. 'For a cut, of course.'

'If I win anythin'.'

'I can't see you've got any competition, mate.'

Ali watched the muscles of Nick's face tighten
confidently into place. 'I'll have to get a stake from
somewhere.'

'That part's your own problem, Ali. I'll do the
rest.'

'Yeah.' Ali swirled his drink. He would have to
try Den again, hit him with the old one about being
on a winner, pointing out that a further loan was his
only chance of getting his money back. Ali fervently
hoped it would work. It hadn't with Doug Fleming.
But then Den wasn't such a bastard as Doug.

When he got back to the café Sue was nursing
another temper flare-up. She let it rip as soon as the
only two customers in the place left.

'Why don't you just walk out on me for good?'
she yelled at Ali. 'I hardly ever see you, anyway. If
I knew you'd buggered off I wouldn't have to
wonder where you are an' what you're up to.'

'What's wrong now?' His hangdog look, he
noticed, was having less and less effect on her these
days. 'I was only round talkin' to a couple of the
suppliers.'

'That's bullshit! They're all shut on a Saturday!'

Ali summoned a rapid comeback. 'Well, yeah – they're shut, but the lads are on the premises. I was makin' enquiries about them new bulk packs of instant mash.'

Sue gathered up the cups and plates from the counter and practically threw them into the sink. 'Save it!' she barked. 'I don't believe a word you say!' She snatched up a sheet of paper from the side of the hotplate and waved it at him. 'While you were out we had a visitor. Somebody who *does* work on a Saturday.'

'Who?'

'The bloody bailiff, that's who.' She thrust the paper into his hand. 'You told me you'd paid the rates, you lyin' sod.'

Ali stared at the paper. Time had a habit of flying when bills were due. There had been a warning through the post, then a threat of court action. Now it seemed the court action had been taken. It had all happened so fast.

'They're goin' to distrain on the furniture,' Sue said. 'Distrain. Know what that means? It means they'll come in here in seven days time an' whip the lot.'

Who said seven was a lucky number, Ali wondered. Seven days to a thumping from Doug's gorillas, seven days to a café without tables or chairs. A lot was hanging on that poker game. He looked at Sue.

'So what're you gonna do?' she demanded.

'Trust me,' he said. 'I'll come up with somethin'.'

28

He watched her, feeling helpless as tears filled her eyes again.

'Well,' Pete said, 'at least I know who they are, now.' He was sitting by the fireside in his mother's house, holding a pocket notebook open on his knee.

Lou put down her knitting and looked at him over the rims of her spectacles. 'An what good's that goin' to do you?'

Pete shrugged. 'I'm not sure, but it feels better to know who the enemy are.'

On two pages of the book were the names of the fourteen traders whose consortium was driving Pete out of business. They were from all over the East End, except two who were based in Fulham. Getting the names and addresses hadn't been easy. Pete had tried for days and had finally discovered – by means which technically constituted breaking and entering – that they were listed on a set of invoices in a dispatch office at New Covent Garden Market.

'They spend thousands of quid a week,' he told Lou. 'It makes a heck of a difference to the prices they can charge. Do you realize I pay nearly twice as much for me sprouts as they do? An' as for apples, bananas an' all the other fruit – well.' He slapped the book shut an put it in his pocket. 'Somethin' drastic's got to be done.'

'How much are you down this week?'

'A lot, Mum . . .'

Lou chewed her lip, reading her son's evasiveness. 'How much is a lot?'

Pete didn't want to tell her. 'We're not on our uppers yet, don't worry about that.'

'But you're eatin' into your savin's, right?'

Pete lowered his head. Lou sat back. Between them they shared a silence that was rich in telepathy. Since childhood, Pete's anxieties and dilemmas had been an open book to his mother, whether he voiced them or not. She could gauge the exact depth of a problem from the smallest of signs. Tonight she felt that her son was in serious trouble.

'Have you any ideas at all? About fightin' back, I mean?'

Pete spread his hands. 'You can only fight this kind of thing with money, Mum. If I spent more than them, I'd be able to sell cheaper than they do. But I can't fight them like that.'

'Is there another way?'

He nodded. 'If you can't fight them, join them. I could try an' get in on the action. That way, at least I could survive. I'd likely get a lot of me old customers back.'

Lou looked doubtful. 'They'd never let you in though, would they?'

'I won't know till I try.' he sighed and stood up. 'I better go an' get me dinner.' He leaned forward and kissed Lou's cheek. 'I'll keep you posted, anyway.'

When he had gone Lou sat and stared at her knitting pattern without seeing it. Troubles came in threes, she thought, they came like trios of big, black, angry crows. By her estimation Pete was staring ruin in the face. Arthur had unemployment coming at him. And her own health was beginning to fail. She had said nothing about that to anyone, not even to her old friend Ethel. There had been sharp, fleeting pains in her chest on and off for a month, and a couple of times she had felt desperately weak and dizzy. Of all the problems, her own worried her most. It wasn't selfishness or self-pity, though. It was the terrible thought that, if anything happened, what would they all do without her?

In the Queen Vic that night Den Watts adopted the manner of a slave master. He kept ordering Angie and Lofty about the place, picking faults, tut-tutting at every turn and urging them to move faster even when they were working flat out. With customers he was bright but abrupt, and although he flurried steadily from one bar to the other, he didn't appear to be doing much.

'He's jumpy about somethin',' Kathy Beale told Pete. They had been sitting at the bar for half an hour, nursing their drinks and hardly speaking, each preoccupied with worries they were too apprehensive to share. 'I can always tell with Den.'

'Yeah, right,' Pete said impatiently. 'So you can tell when somebody's jumpy. Great.'

Kathy glared at him. 'What are you snappin' at me for? I was only sayin' – '

'I heard what you said.'

'Pardon me for breathin'.' Kathy picked up her glass, then put it down again without taking a drink. 'It's always the same when we've got money worries, isn't it? You get all shirty with me. It isn't fair. I'm just as upset about it as you are.'

'We've got more than straightforward money worries this time,' Pete muttered. 'This is the big one. Bankruptcy.'

'It's still no excuse to pick on me. An' anyway,

we're nowhere near bankrupt. You're always exaggeratin'.'

Pete turned slowly on his stool and looked at her. 'Nowhere near, eh? We're doin' practically no business. But I've still got to buy fresh stock every day, just in case trade turns better. At the end of each day I've got to sling most of what I've bought that mornin'. Now how long do you think we can carry on that way without goin' broke?' He turned away again and stared at the rows of bottles on the rack fitting.

Angie came along the bar and tapped Kathy's arm. 'Cheer up. It might never happen.'

'Sorry,' Kathy said. 'I'm lookin' that bad, am I?'

'Like you'd found out sex is ruinin' your health.' Angie glanced at Den, who was taking change from the till. 'Don't suppose you've any idea what's up with my old man? He's behavin' very odd tonight.'

'I'd noticed.'

'He's up to somethin', I reckon.'

'Well,' Kathy murmured, 'if we both keep watchin' him, we're bound to find out what it is.'

By ten-thirty Den was more agitated than ever. In the space of five minutes he managed to short-change one customer and give another one the wrong drink. He had broken a glass, knocked a bottle off its optic stand and spilled Ethel's Guinness all over the bar towel. He was mopping up the mess when Lofty decided to approach him on a delicate matter.

'Erm, Den, can I have a word?'

'If you're quick.' Den took the bar towel to the sink and began wringing it out. Lofty followed him.

'It's about my shift next Friday.' He cleared his throat nervously. 'I wondered if I could change it to another night. Just for the one week, of course.'

Den slapped the towel down on the drainer. 'Friday's a night when I need you,' he pointed out, scarcely parting his teeth. 'What do you want to change for?'

'This, um, drivin' an' deliverin' job I'm doin' – the bloke wants me to do some evenin' deliveries next Friday.'

'We can't have everythin' we want, Lofty.'

'It's just the once, Den.'

'You said that already.' Den glanced along the bar. Three people were waiting to be served. 'Look, get movin' before we lose half our punters. You can ask me about the Friday evenin' business again at closin' time.'

As Lofty shuffled off Pete Beale leaned over the counter. 'Den, you haven't got an aspirin, have you?'

'Yeah, I think so.' He squinted at Pete. 'What's the matter? You look a bit peaky.'

'I think I've managed to split my head with worryin'.'

'Business still goin' down?'

Pete nodded wearily.

'I know just the thing for your achin' bonce. Aspirin's for cissies.' He went to the far end of the back shelf and brought back a bottle of Fernet Branca. 'This'll even stop you worryin' for a bit.' He poured a measure into a liqueur glass. 'There. It's on the house.' He sighed as Pete sank the drink. 'I'm not feelin' too bright meself tonight. Between you an' me, I think I made a grave error of judgement earlier this evenin'.'

Pete made a face as the liquid burned its way to his stomach. 'How do you mean?'

'I let Ali borrow fifty off me.'

'Bad move.'

'I'm beginnin' to think that. But at the time it seemed sound enough – an' I was sorry for him. He wanted to get into a game an' he needed the stake.'

'Bloody hell. It'd take more than pity to make me lend a bloke money to gamble with.'

'It's a safe game, accordin' to him, but as the night's wore on, I've been thinkin' to meself I've kissed that bundle goodbye.' Den sucked his teeth thoughtfully. 'Ali was too nervous to play on his top form. I've been clobbered at poker by dummies meself, when I wasn't in the right frame of mind.'

'Dear, dear. So maybe you'll be fifty down by mornin', eh?'

Den shook his head slowly. 'More than that. This money was loaned to try an' get him out of a bad financial fix – an' to get back the last fifty I gave him.'

Pete looked astonished. 'What's gettin' into you? You're turnin' *charitable* in your middle age, for God's sake. That just ain't your style at all.'

Much later, when the pub was closed, when Angie had gone upstairs and Lofty had gone home with the promise, grudgingly given, that he could work next Thursday instead of Friday, Den sat down in the bar with a large brandy. He would give Ali until midnight, he decided, then he would go to bed and sleep on the certainty that the money was lost.

34

It was odd, he mused, that although he regretted lending the money, he still didn't feel any rancour towards Ali. They were both gamblers and they shared a zest for the special risks of a poker game. It had been the idea of being involved in a game, if only by providing the stake, that had made Den finally hand over the cash. He sipped his brandy slowly and wondered at it. Gambling and women, the two most hazardous pursuits in the world, seemed to be the only ones that really fired him. He was wondering if Ali ever got the urge for any other woman when there was a loud banging on the side door.

He put down his glass and went across. 'Who is it?'

Somebody mumbled something. It sounded like a drunk.

'What?'

This time he heard clearly. It was Ali. Den unbolted the door and pulled it open. 'Jesus wept!' Ali was leaning on the door jamb. There was a caked stream of blood on his face, running from his hairline to his chin. One of his jacket sleeves was missing. 'What happened?'

'Let me in,' Ali panted. 'I've run about a soddin' mile.'

'Come on. I'll give you a hand. Mind you don't get blood on me shirt.' Den led him to the table and pointed at the brandy glass. 'Sit down an' get that inside you.' He closed the door, went behind the bar for two fresh brandies then came back and sat down opposite Ali. 'Tell me the worst. You can have a wash an' tidy in the bog when you've finished.'

'The game went all right,' Ali said. He was still breathless. 'I could see they were useless right from the start. So I let a couple of them win, an' I folded a couple of times when I didn't need to.' He dabbed at his bruised lips with his cuff.

'And?' Den prompted.

'I cleaned up. Took the whole pot.' He went silent again, gulping for air.

'Go on,' Den said grimly.

'It was when I got out of the place, the club where we were playin'. The Pakis had took it badly, losin' all that dough, but I didn't think they'd get violent or nothin'. But they'd two big lads waitin' for me.'

'Oh, shit,' Den groaned.

'They really worked me over. The pains are comin' on all over me, now I've stopped runnin'.' He pulled open his jacket. 'See – they tore out all me pockets. Even the trouser ones.'

Den's expression was moving from shocked to glum. 'How much did they get?'

Ali moved his lips painfully. Den thought he was going to be sick, then realized he was trying to smile.

'They got nothin'. Why'd you think I had to run for it?' He tugged open his trousers and reached down inside. 'I nipped into the loo before I left. Good job I was wearin' underpants with elastic in the legs, eh?' He drew out a thick wad of money and slapped it on the table. 'Mind you,' he gasped, 'I nearly wrecked me weddin' tackle, runnin' with that lot down me crutch.'

Den stared at the money, feeling relief wash over him. There had to be about eight or nine hundred there. He looked up at Ali, who was laughing painfully.

'Not bad, eh, Den?'

A big grin spread across Den's face. 'Not bad at all, Ali me old mate.' He leaned across and hugged the bloodstained little man, his heart swelling with the love of one true gambler for another.

March

'Something very lucky's going to happen for you,' Ethel said. She was gazing intently at the right palm of Debbie Wilkins, who was trying not to look embarrassed. Debbie's boyfriend Andy stood alongside, openly amused.

'I'm taking a banking exam soon,' Debbie murmured. 'Maybe it's something to do with that.' She was never sure if she believed in this kind of thing or not. 'Can you be more specific?'

'I'll try, dear.' Ethel's habit of grabbing passers-by and telling their fortunes was commonplace in Bridge Street. Market shoppers and stallholders regarded her as part of the day to day activity. Very few had escaped her attention over the years, but this was Debbie's first reading. 'I definitely see money.' Ethel peered closer. 'Yes, it's connected with money.'

'Amazing,' Andy said.

Ethel released Debbie's hand and smiled up at her. 'There, I'm sure that's brightened your day.' She moved closer, still smiling, which was more persuasive than actually asking for money.

'Oh.' Debbie fumbled for her purse and opened it. 'Thanks very much.' She held out a fifty pence piece.

'Oh, you shouldn't . . .' Ethel snatched the coin and put it in her pocket. 'Do you know somethin'?

I'm sure you'll stay lucky.' She patted Debbie's elbow. 'You've got that special aura.' She turned aside, spotting a stranger by Pete Beale's stall. 'Must be goin', then. Things to do.'

As Ethel homed-in on the new target Andy put his arm around Debbie. 'Isn't it nice to know you've got an aura, eh?' The Scottish burr put an extra edge of irony in his voice. 'Here's me been thinking it was the deodorant you used, when all along it was a lucky halo hanging round you.'

'Don't mock,' Debbie said irritably. 'It's supposed to be bad luck to make fun of fortune-tellers.'

'Only if they're big and hairy and happen to hear you doing it.' Andy looked at his watch, then nodded towards the door of The Vic. 'We've got an hour yet before the towels go up. Fancy a drinkie?'

Debbie wrinkled her nose; it was one of her armoury of facial signals; it meant that she wanted to have her own way, without being publicly adamant about it. 'I want to take this lamb home and get it into the marinade.' Saturdays were valuable to her. They were the only times when she could play housewife properly, starting with the shopping, then preparing the next day's dinner, then doing some cleaning and polishing before going out for the evening.

'I really fancy a drink,' Andy said.

Debbie shrugged. 'You go and have a pint if you want to. I'll have a glass of wine while I'm pottering about in the kitchen.'

Andy understood these blackmail notes – he had to cope with two or three a week. Debbie was now saying that she wanted to go home and that she would prefer him to come with her, for she liked him to be around and pass admiring remarks as she demonstrated her culinary flair. If he chose to have a pint instead of going straight home, then there would be a small but distinct chill between them for the rest of the day, and he could forget any ideas of having his usual Saturday-night thrash under the duvet.

Today, Andy felt like having a drink, whatever the consequences. 'You carry on then, love,' he said. 'I'll see you about ten to three.'

Debbie nodded stiffly and let him kiss her cheek before she walked away. Andy turned towards the pub, inhaling its beery breath as the door swung open to let an unsteady citizen out. He did enough for peace, he reflected, catching the door. He had no cause for self-reproach in that area. Debbie had her idea of a domestic pattern and so had he. The one feature hers lacked was compromise. He stepped into the bar, reminding himself that if he had enough to drink, he would scarcely notice the atmosphere at home.

'Whoops!' He almost collided with Lofty, who was backing away from the bar. 'Steady, mate. You're supposed to face the way you're going.'

Lofty apologized elaborately with his hands. 'Sorry, I just remembered I'm supposed to be somewhere.'

Den leaned across the bar. 'Oi! Remember – five-thirty on the dot tonight. That don't mean twenty to six.'

'I'll be here,' Lofty promised, then to Andy he said, 'It's a lot of hassle, havin' two jobs.'

'How's the other one going?'

'Great.' Lofty pushed his glasses up on his nose, where they remained for a moment before sliding down again. 'The money's good an' I'm gettin' busier all the time. But now an' again I get dead harassed. Like now.' He gave an unconvincing thumbs-up to Den and pushed open the door. 'See you, Andy.'

He was approximately ten minutes late. To get to the lockup where the van was housed would take him another five. He began running as he got under the railway bridge, remembering not to overdo it in case he brought on an asthma attack. The delivery was in Notting Hill, so with a bit of luck he could plead heavy traffic holdups when he finally arrived there.

Panting, he got to the lockup and opened the heavy padlock. The Transit was just where he had left it, which always surprised him a little. He clambered into the cab, checked his consignment through the hatch, then started the engine. The delivery address was on the clipboard beside him. He had delivered there once before and knew the route. He took the van out, locked up again and headed towards the river.

Driving was a soothing job. It gave him time to think and there was nobody around to keep shoving him, the way Den and Angie did. Over the past few weeks Lofty had decided that if he ever could, he would take a permanent transport-and-delivery job. Then he would pack in working in the pub and get himself away from physical supervision for good.

It was especially calming to pass by Saturday

crowds in the insulation of the van, seeing them without having to be a part of their togetherness, without even having to steer round them the way he hated doing when he was on foot. If somebody spoke to Lofty on the street they put a strain on him, a taxing necessity to respond and become part of a two- or three-way transaction. He liked people and he found it pleasant to be among them, if they would only leave him alone. He was content to be a spectator.

'Hyde and Rowbotham,' he murmured, glancing at the name on the clipboard and thinking how much they sounded like a firm of solicitors, or estate agents. In fact they were two pretty surly individuals, one of them a Yorkshireman, who had a shadowy big warehouse packed with crates and cartons with well-known names on them like Smirnoff, Hoover, Hitachi, EMI. In fact the only boxes that had no markings at all were the ones Lofty delivered. They were always the same: plain, white, measuring three feet by two by about four inches deep, and they were always stapled shut. Lofty had no idea what they contained. On the single occasion he asked, he had been told it was none of his business.

The secrecy was the only unsettling feature of the job. Now and then it made him edgy, ferrying round boxes of something he never saw and never heard named. He couldn't believe everything was straight and above-board; the secrecy was one reason for his suspicion, the fact that Nick Cotton got him the job was another, but the strongest cause for believing he was an accessory to some kind of skulduggery was the boss himself. Barry French had villain stamped all over him. From the three-inch forehead and hooded, slow-blinking eyes, to the tattooed knuckles and his habit of fingering his mouth when he spoke, the man oozed shiftiness and criminal intent.

'Just keep your nose clean, son, do what your told, an' you'll get on just fine.' That had been his introductory instruction to Lofty. Since then he had hardly uttered another complete sentence to him.

As he drove across Lambeth Bridge Lofty began to wonder about Barry again. What business was he in? The few acquaintances of Lofty's who had heard of him had no idea what he did. He operated from a third-floor office on the east boundary of Walford and seemed to employ a transient staff of hangers-on. There was also a girl who looked too dim to operate the typewriter she sat behind in the ante-room. The sign on the door said B. FRENCH ENTERPRISES. Enterprise seemed particularly lacking in the office; nobody appeared to do more than hang around drinking coffee and smoking. The girl shifted bits of paper from time to time and occasionally Lofty had heard Barry muttering into the telephone. The boxes he had to deliver were always stacked in one corner, set out in groups of five and six with delivery times and addresses attached to the top carton of each pile. What *were* they?

Lofty glanced over his shoulder into the back of the van. The anonymous boxes swayed innocently, telling him nothing. He returned his eyes to the road ahead, knowing he shouldn't be curious at all. Nick had warned him not to be. But it was intriguing all the same. A person couldn't help being a shade curious, after all. It was only human.

By the time he reached Notting Hill he had managed to make up a few minutes by taking back turnings and avoiding the busier roads. Nevertheless, Messrs Hyde and Rowbotham looked disgruntled as he pulled up outside their warehouse.

'Where the bloody hell have you been, pal? We've been hangin' on here like a pair of lemons.' Hyde was small and tightly aggressive, like a hyperactive monkey. He jerked his thumb towards an outbuilding as Lofty stepped down. 'Get the stuff out double quick an' stack it inside the door there.'

Lofty discarded the excuse he had prepared and began unloading. As he carried the boxes across the yard the tight-lipped figure of Rowbotham shadowed him, like a guard monitoring a shipment of gold. This was something else that intrigued Lofty. These men, in common with the others he visited, acted like the recipients of something precious yet dangerous, to be promptly locked up before they retired to a safe distance. Nobody ever stayed near the boxes for long.

As he put down the second stack he noticed something. In the far corner of the outhouse there was an opened carton, identical to the ones he had brought. Nestling in the bottom was something oblong and black. Lofty blinked across at it, wondering.

'Right.' Rowbotham tapped his shoulder. 'That's the lot. You can get moving again.' He virtually pushed Lofty out of the building and slammed the door shut.

As he clambered into the van and started up the engine, Lofty watched Hyde put on the two security padlocks as Rowbotham stood by with the keys. After a moment he realized he was staring, and Rowbotham was staring back at him.

It's none of your business, Lofty told himself sharply. He grinned weakly and waved as he pulled out of the yard.

On 8th March the Social Services Secretary, Mr Fowler, announced that National Health prescription charges would be increased by twenty pence per item from mid April.

'One way an' another,' Lou Beale told Ethel, as they had an afternoon cup of tea in the front room, 'I've good reason to get the hump every time I hear the name Fowler. There's one up there in Parliament rookin' the poor every chance he gets, an' another one under me own roof that can't look out for his own wife an' family.'

Ethel thought that was unfair. 'Arthur can't help losin' his job,' she pointed out. 'It's not as if he's gettin' fired for bein' a shirker or nothin' like that. He's bein' made *redundant*, isn't he?'

'So? He's had plenty of time to find another job – the writin's been on the wall for long enough.'

'It's hard at his age,' Ethel sighed.

'He don't know that till he's tried.' Lou rapped the table irritably. 'That's what's put me back up, Et. He hasn't even tried. He's stood still an' let disaster happen to him, instead of takin' precautions. He's got no bloody go in him. Never had.'

Ethel still thought it was unfair. If Lou had a

religion, it was founded in her strong belief in action. According to her creed, people had to create circumstances; they couldn't simply expect things to happen for them.

'If he'd any spine at all, he'd have been out every spare minute he'd got, drummin' up a job. It's what a man's supposed to do, isn't it? He's meant to provide. He's got to make the effort.'

That was fair enough as far as it went, Ethel thought, but there was a lot the principle didn't take into account. Arthur Fowler was a kind, caring, warm human being. He was of a gentle breed that found it hard to take fortune by the horns, but he was also a nicer person than a lot who did find it easy. Although she wouldn't pursue the point with Lou, Ethel believed that what was important was not Arthur's lack of drive, but the fact that he possessed charm. That was scarce nowadays.

'Maybe he has been tryin', Lou.'

'Oh, he says he has.'

'There you are, then . . .'

'But he's lyin',' Lou growled. 'I can always tell when he is. His eyes start wobblin' about an' he can't look you in the face.' She sipped her tea as if it were something bitter. 'There's poor Pauline slavin' away in that launderette every afternoon to make a few quid, an' me havin' to feed the kids when they get in from school. What'll his lordship be doin' when they pay him off at the end of the month? Spendin' his redundancy money over in The Vic every dinner time, I'll bet, an' then sleepin' it off all afternoon.'

'Oh, I'm sure it won't be like that, love . . .'

46

'He's a lazy bugger,' Lou said flatly. 'I can see it now. He's most likely been that way all along. I mean, we don't know what kind of work he's been doin' over the years, do we? Maybe he makes the tea at the factory. Maybe he just sweeps up. It's the men what do important jobs that get kept on, isn't it?'

Ethel felt she should go. Otherwise there was a real danger she would fall out with Lou. She put down her cup and saucer and stood up. 'Come on, Willie.' Her pug dog jumped on to the chair and she gathered him into her arms. 'Best thing you can do,' she told Lou, 'is have yourself another cuppa and get your mind on to somethin' else. Frettin's bad for you – an' it gets you nowhere.'

Lou went to the kitchen with Ethel and pulled open the back door. 'I'd get me mine on somethin' else if there wasn't so flamin' much worryin' me.'

Ethel nodded. 'You've got a lot on your plate, I'll say that. How's things with Pete, anyway?'

'No better. He's puttin' a brave face on it, but I can tell business is gettin' worse all the time. You only have to look at his barrow at knockin' off time.' Lou's yard door opened on to Bridge Street, opposite Pete's stall. 'He brings me in more veg than I know what to do with. The rest he throws away. It's terrible. Terrible.' She took a sudden deep breath and squared her shoulders. 'Still *he's* tryin' to do somethin' about his troubles. He's a fighter our Pete. A proper Beale, just like his Dad.'

When Ethel had gone Lou went back to the front room and stared out of the window. Across the square she saw Reg Cox, the scruffiest, most anti-social element in the district, shuffling his way up the steps at number 23. For a moment she wondered uncharitably if Arthur would end up like that, a shambling scrounger that even dogs couldn't take to, a leech on the community whose only value was to remind people where idleness would get them. There was a swift, unbidden vision of her own son Pete in exactly the same condition. She thrust the image aside and went back to the table and the teapot.

'It's turnin' out a rotten old country we live in, Albert.' She spoke to her dead husband a lot lately, usually to pass on dispatches from the grim, breathing world. 'We've got nothin' but strikes, riots, inflation, redundancies, IRA bombs – an' Thatcher. You're not missin' a lot of fun, me love.'

These days, Lou never seemed able to divert her attention from something gloomy to something cheerful; the only alternative to gloom now was something less gloomy. In the old days life had been tough enough, it had been downright terrible at times, but there had been a lot of happiness too, a lot of light and warmth.

'Those were the days,' she murmured as she poured the tea. 'Folks liked each other more.'

The overall quality of life, from the late sixties on, had seemed to Lou to become more harsh, often barbarous. Only the day before, she had read in her *Daily Mirror* about two Hell's Angels who had knifed a boy to death in front of his girlfriend, then tied her to a tree and strangled her with her own scarf. Eight days before Christmas, a terrorist bomb went off behind Harrods; it killed six people and maimed dozens more. People had been found starving in the East End, pensioners were regularly robbed and beaten up, there were endless stories of children being raped, tortured and murdered. Maybe things like that had happened in the past, Lou thought, but they had never happened on such a scale.

She sat down and picked up her cup. It was halfway to her lips when a sharp pain gripped her chest, making her fingers clench and spill the tea across the tablecloth. Lou dropped the cup and pushed herself to her feet, panting for breath, leaning on the table for support.

'Oh, my good God . . .'

The pain went as swiftly as it came. It left her weak and gasping. When she felt she could make it, she got herself to the kitchen and poured a glass of water. Her hands shook so badly she had to wrap them both around the tumbler before she could take a drink.

'That felt close, Albert,' she whispered. It had been weeks since the last pain. She had even dared to hope they had left her for good. 'It's all this worryin',' she panted. 'That's what's doin' it.'

She went into the living room and sat down on the couch. One piece of good news, she thought, would change everything. Even a ray of hope would be a tonic for her. She leaned back and closed her eyes, willing her heart – or whatever it was – to behave itself and hang on for a touch of brightness on the horizon.

That evening, Pete Beale went to a pub in Islington to meet a man called Charlie Brandon. It was a meeting that had taken a long time to arrange. Brandon was an organizing member of the consortium that had now practically beggared Pete and his family. Not surprisingly, Brandon hadn't especially wanted the meeting. He could see no advantage in Pete's proposition. Over their first drink he told Pete that again.

'I'm only here to get the matter settled once an' for all, Mr Beale. Then maybe you'll stop pesterin' me on the blower.'

They were leaning on the rounded corner of the bar, Brandon with his face turned towards the others in the room, Pete trying to look squarely at him. It wasn't an easy face to look at, even obliquely. Brandon was a veteran of the Korean war. In the fifties, after less than two years' service, he had come home for good, invalided out at the age of twenty with a face hideously scarred by petrol burns. From above the mouth the face was a taut, mottled, shiny mask, incapable of expression. When his mouth opened the scar tissue tightened even more, making his lower eyelids dip and reveal the red orbital tissue.

'I thought a meetin' might help to convince you,' Pete said. 'I can be an asset. I'm not askin' for charity.'

Brandon sighed and sipped his beer. Drinking was a delicate operation, requiring him to curl his bottom lip firmly round the glass to compensate for the absence of grip in the thin, fleshless upper lip.

When he had managed to swallow a couple of ounces he put the glass down again.

'I've told you already. We're precisely the size we need to be. Our number of outlets is carefully keyed to our purchasing power. The profit-sharing has been worked out just as carefully.'

'Are you sayin' one more trader, puttin' in his proper whack every week, is goin' to upset the balance?'

'I'm sayin' we don't need to find out.'

Pete would have preferred to convince Brandon on the one-more-makes-no-difference argument. But there wasn't even a hand-hold there. From a businessman's standpoint Brandon was right – why should he go to the trouble? Pete moved on to his second approach, an appeal to the man's humanity.

'I've been practically driven out of business,' he said. 'It's obvious why. Now don't get me wrong. I don't want to come the bleedin' heart, but there's somethin' to be said for tradition. My dad was runnin' that fruit an' veg stall before the war. My mum kept it goin' for as long as she could durin' the war years. Then Dad took it up again when he came back – '

'Sure, sure,' Brandon interrupted. 'I know all about that.'

'But if you'd look at it from the family point of view – I mean, really see what the business means to us.' It occurred to Pete that it might be harder getting sympathy from a mutilated ex-soldier than it would from an ordinary man. But he had to try. 'What I'm sayin' is a man in your position, with your clout in the trade, could surely make a concession that'd cost you nothin', just to keep a bit of our good old East End tradition flourishin'.'

Brandon turned and stared at him. The curl of his lip was as expressive as a whole faceful of muscles. 'Mr Beale,' he said quietly, 'I'd take it kindly if you wouldn't hit me with that Cockney brotherhood shit.'

'I was only suggestin' – '

'Listen. The people that've done me the most dirt in my business career – I mean the really wicked, underhanded, evil, back-stabbin' bastards – have all been sons of the good old East End.'

Pete realized this meeting had been stillborn. He had less chance of joining the consortium than he had of winning the ITV Seven. To satisfy himself that he had tried his best, though, he made one more pitch.

'Look, I'll put it to you straight. I'm askin' you to save me bacon. Without your help, I'm sunk.'

Brandon shook his head slowly. 'I'm sorry, Mr Beale. Even if I'd wanted to let you in, I couldn't. You've got a serious enemy on our team.'

Pete thought hard for a moment. There hadn't been a name on that list that he had known. 'Who? He's got to be he's mistakin' me for somebody else . . .'

'No mistake. The firm of T F Jennings and Sons wants no dealin's with you, at any price.'

'But I don't know them,' Pete protested. 'I've never dealt with them in me life.'

'The tradin' name is an old one,' Brandon said. 'The actual owner's name is Geoffrey Harris.'

For a long moment it meant nothing to Pete, then light dawned, sharp and clear. Geoff Harris. He was a brother of Pat Harris, who had been Pete's first wife.

'Christ. I haven't set eyes on him for years.'

'With him, the memory lingers on. I wouldn't want too many people hatin' me that hard.'

It had been so long ago it seemed to Pete like another life. At the time he had left Pat, her family had actively blackened his name around Walford and created as much vindictive mischief as they could. Geoff, in particular, had campaigned hard on his sister's behalf. He had found her the hot-shot lawyer who put Pete through a financial mangle for years after the divorce. In an angry letter to Pete, Geoff had once promised he would never miss an opportunity to do him harm.

'I didn't even know he was in the veg business,' Pete said bleakly.

'Nearly ten years. He's been pretty successful, too.' Brandon drank some more of his beer then pushed the glass away. 'I'll have to be goin' home.' He turned to Pete. 'We've had our meetin', just like you wanted. I hope you understand how things stand now.'

Pete nodded. 'Yeah. It's clear as bloody crystal.'

Brandon left without another word. Pete set his elbows on the bar and stared at his glass. Since the time he married Kathy, nearly fifteen years ago, he had thought his past life, his tortured life with Pat, was a dead thing. It had diminished to no more than the husks of old memories, no longer painful. He had believed nothing from that time could hurt him ever again. But it was still there, the living, vigorous power of that family's hatred. It had reached out and cut him again.

He finished his drink and ordered another pint. There was no way he could face going home sober. 'Give me a scotch with it an' all, love, will you?'

Ten minutes later he began to feel a little more numb. There was the beginning of resignation, too. He had tried everything. Now it was up to fate. The attempt to get into the consortium had been a hopeless move. Even without Geoff Harris's veto, there would still have been no chance, not if Charlie Brandon's manner had been any guide. But he had tried, Pete reminded himself, he had made a positive, if desperate effort to get himself out of the muck. But he was stuck and that was that.

'Bollocks to it.'

He swallowed the dregs of his beer and moved away from the bar. Outside he stopped suddenly as the cold air hit him.

'You stupid tit,' he told himself.

It was all very well feeling resigned when he only had his own skin to look out for. But what about Kathy and young Ian? What about family, home, the future? A chill of anxiety seeped through him again. He turned up his coat collar and strode across to the van. There had to be something else to try, he thought as he jerked open the door. There just had to be *something*.

Mark Fowler was fifteen. In terms of experience he was rather older. He had been smoking on a casual basis for more than a year and on three occasions he had been drunk. Sex and gambling had also figured in his social learning, but until Nick Cotton put a proposition to him one Friday night at the end of March, he'd had no personal involvement with drugs.

'It's the propaganda that's got everybody screwed up about this stuff,' Nick said. He was leaning on the wall by the telephone box in the corner of the square. In his hand he had a small foil package. He hefted it like a stubby bullet and held it out to Mark. 'Give it a try.'

Mark had slow-moving features. They took about ten seconds to register his reluctance as he stared at the packet. 'I don't know, Nick . . .'

'It's OK. I wouldn't let you have anythin' harmful.'

'I've heard some stories about cannabis.'

'An' I've heard a tale or two about fags an' beer an' even Coca Cola. It's propaganda. Lies. All them stories are put about by cranks.' He edged closer. 'Look at me. Do I look like a crazed drug fiend? I smoke this all the time an' it don't do me no harm at all.'

'But you can get hooked . . .'

'Nah.' Nick made a disparaging face as he unwrapped the brown waxy chunk. 'I can show you books, serious books, that tell you this stuff ain't habit formin'. We're not talkin' about glue-sniffin' or acid trippin' or anythin' dangerous like that. Listen. If hash had been discovered before tobacco, all the fags would made from it an' snout would be illegal.'

Mark took the lump and rolled it between his fingers. 'What does it do to you?'

'Makes you feel great. Not a care in the world. It'll let you see the funny side of everythin' – even your old man gettin' booted out of his job.' Nick produced a packet of cigarette papers. 'I'll roll us up a joint, eh?' He nodded towards the wall beyond the telephone box. 'Round there. Won't take a minute.'

Mark frowned. 'What'll it cost? I've not much bread on me.'

'It's free,' Nick said, winking. 'If you don't fancy it, well, it's no skin off my arse. If you do, then I can always get you some – an' I'm cheaper than anybody else around here.'

Mark shrugged and followed Nick behind the wall. He had never needed much persuading when it came to overstepping convention. In the slanting light from the street he watched as four papers were deftly gummed together and the tobacco from two cigarettes was spread in a thick line along the middle.

'Got to cook it a bit,' Nick explained as he held the flame of his lighter to the piece of resin. 'It's economical, hash is. Doesn't take much to do the trick.' He crumbled the blackened portion on to the tobacco, pocketed the lump and rolled the paper into a tube, carefully twisting one end. 'There.' He held it up with some pride. 'Let's have a blast, eh?'

At that moment, fifty yards away in The Vic, Mark's father was starting on his sixth pint. At the table with him were his wife Pauline, his mother-in-law and Ethel Skinner. Of the four, only Arthur appeared to be enjoying himself.

'He'll be up sick for half the night,' Lou grunted to Ethel. She threw Arthur a look of open distaste.

56

'I've never known him have more than four pints, even at Christmas.'

'He's entitled to drown his sorrows,' Ethel said.

'Looks like they're dead an' gone long ago, from the daft grin on his face.'

Arthur was pursuing a line he decided on as soon as he had known he would be made redundant. Tonight was the zone of demarcation between security and insecurity. It would be a time of mind-wiping, of washing himself right into the condition called Unemployment. 'There'll be time enough for moanin' an' worryin',' he had told Pauline as they got ready to leave the house. 'Tonight, we'll blow a few quid of me severance money in The Vic. We'll have a good time an' we'll make sure it *is* a good time, since it's likely to be the last one we'll have.'

It was fortunate that the beer had dulled Arthur's awareness of the atmosphere at the table. Lou had been grumpy since they arrived. Ethel was apprehensive, in case Lou started laying into Arthur, and Pauline simply couldn't get over her foreboding, although she was behaving as brightly as she could.

'I'll have a terrible head tomorrow,' Arthur said, grinning. 'I must say it feels great right now, though.' He patted Pauline's hand. 'Come on, love, you're not drinkin'.' He switched his attention to Lou, who was scowling at the air above his head. 'How's about us havin' a sing-song Mum, eh?' Without waiting for a response, he launched straight into the chorus of *My Old Man's a Dustman*. Pauline joined in and Ethel tried to, but Lou nudged her sharply.

'Don't encourage the silly sod,' she hissed.

Den was watching Arthur from behind the bar. 'I

don't get it,' he said to Angie. 'The bloke's just been turfed out of work, he's got no prospects of ever findin' another job, an' yet he's goin' on like his ship's just come in.'

'It has,' Angie said. 'Two thousand quid's more money than Arthur's ever had in his hands before.'

'It won't last him long.'

Angie shrugged. 'Maybe he doesn't want it to. I keep hearin' about them redundancy parties, with blokes blowin' all their pay-off money in one gigantic bash at the local.'

Den nodded, remembering one or two men of his acquaintance who had thrown away their money because the prospect of it dwindling was too suspenseful and too painful to live with. He recalled, too, that his grannie, a very poor old woman, had once told him it was terrible to have just a little of anything left. She would always put her last few shillings on a horse, rather than hang on to it.

'I don't think that's what Arthur's doin' though, Angie. He's not the squanderin' type.'

'Well, whatever he's up to he looks happy enough, bless him.' She turned and took up her usual smiling position at the bar as the doors swung open. Ali and Sue Osman came in. Angie took one look, sized up their mood and held on tightly to her smile. 'Hello, you two. How's it goin', then?'

Ali made a face that he was careful not to let his wife see. 'As well as can be expected,' he muttered.

Sue slumped on to a stool beside him, her face a study in discontent. 'We've just been to have a look at what the Council calls accommodation,' she told

Angie. 'I've seen animals in better quarters up at Whipsnade.'

'Aw, it ain't that bad,' Ali protested.

'It's horrible.'

Angie asked them what property they had viewed.

'The groundfloor flat at number twenty-three,' Sue said. 'You know, one of the classier residences in Albert Square. Christ.' She shook her head as if she still couldn't believe what she had seen. 'It's pokey, it's filthy an' it stinks.' She glared at Ali, as if it were his fault. 'We know why it stinks, don't we?'

Angie's smile had gone. 'Reg Cox,' she said. 'God, I wouldn't like livin' anywhere with him on the premises.'

'He's not just livin' upstairs,' Sue pointed out. 'We'd be expected to share the bathroom with him. An' you should just *see* the bathroom.'

Ali was waving his hand gently, trying to disperse her revulsion. 'You're over-reactin', love.'

'No I'm not.'

'But you are. With a good clean through an' a lick of paint, that place would look just fine.'

'Listen.' Sue jabbed a finger at him. 'If you think I'm puttin' my bum on a toilet seat that's had Reg Cox's on it, you've got another think comin'.'

'At least the bathtub won't have seen much use,' Angie murmured. 'Did the Council offer you anythin' else?'

Sue nodded. 'Can't say they didn't give us a lot of choice. It's either number twenty-three, or a vandalized top-floor wind tunnel two miles away, or a bug hutch in Carver Road.'

'The one in the square's the best of the lot,' Ali said. 'It's handy for the café an' right bang among a lot of people we know.'

'Includin' Reg Cox,' Sue snapped.

Ali ordered the drinks from Angie and turned to Sue again. 'We've got to make up our minds by Monday. If we turn down the lot, we won't get offered anythin' again for ages.'

'I don't want to think about it.'

'But you have to.'

'Tomorrow,' Sue said. 'I'll think about it then, when I'm not feelin' so bloody upset.'

It had occurred to Ali that he was never out of trouble, not even with his bills paid and money in his pocket. There had been a time, long before he was married, when life had been carefree, an easy jaunt from one experience to the next. He couldn't blame Sue for the change. He had wanted to marry her and she had made him happier than he would have been if she had said no. But the troubles had piled up since they had become man and wife. Marriage itself was the problem, it imposed extra responsibility and the need to lead a more orderly life. That was a sad truth to face; in chasing happiness he had landed himself – in fact both of them – with a lapful of woes.

He reached out and touched Sue's shoulder. 'I'll make it all work out for us, love.' He watched her scowling face as she picked up her drink. 'I promise you.'

Sue looked at him. 'I'll tell you something,' she said, almost whispering. 'I wish more an' more, every day, that I wasn't havin' this baby.'

'Don't say that.'

'It's true. If I'd not fallen pregnant, we wouldn't be in this mess. We'd still be able to stay at your dad's an' get on with buildin' up the business. A baby's just goin' to be a millstone round our necks. It's goin' to foul up everything.'

Ali couldn't argue with that. But he wouldn't agree with it, either. He tightened his fingers on her shoulder. 'This is the way things were intended to go, darlin'. We've got to make the best of what we're handed.'

'Oh God,' Sue groaned. 'So it's fate now, is it?'

'Yeah. I reckon it is. An' you can't fight it.'

'There's nothin' to stop me hatin' it.'

Ali sighed and gave Angie the money for the drinks. She took it and smiled at Sue. 'Cheer up,' she said. 'Nothin's as bad as it seems at first sight.'

'Oh yeah?' Sue got off the stool and walked away to a table in the corner. Ali shrugged and followed her. As they sat down Pete Beale came in.

'Has Rob Burkett been in?' he asked Angie.

She thought for a moment. 'I don't think I know him – do I?'

'Of course you do.' Pete held up a hand at chest height. 'He's a tichy little bloke, broad as he's long, with mutton-chop whiskers.'

'Oh, *him*. No, I ain't seen him for ages, love.'

'Damn.' Pete edged on to a stool. 'I've been lookin' for him all over.'

Den came forward. 'Robbie Burkett, did you say? He was in for a packet of fags earlier. Said he was goin' straight off on a long-distance job.'

'Great.' Pete planted his elbows on the bar. 'I might as well stop an' have a pint, then.'

Angie moved away as Den pulled the drink. 'Was it important, then?' he asked Pete.

'I'll say. I wanted to take him up on an offer he made me about six months ago.'

Den nodded as he put the pint in front of Pete. 'He's a generous little fella, Robbie. Always offerin' to do somebody a favour.'

'This one could save my skin.' Pete took a swallow and put the glass down again. 'He's got this haulage business, as you know. There's a van he hardly ever uses because it's too small for most of his ordinary jobs an' too big for small contracts. He offered to let me use it for a couple of months, rent-free.'

'What for?'

'He had this notion that if I tried street-to-street sellin', I'd do better. At the time I thought it was a daft idea. I suddenly remembered the offer this afternoon – an' now I think different. I mean, what've I got to lose?'

'Not a lot, from what you've been tellin' me lately.'

'Before the slump set in, I didn't want to change. But I'm finished on the market now – or I will be soon. I reckon with a bit of effort I could make a go of sellin' round the houses.'

'It'd give you an edge,' Den agreed. 'Is your own van no good?'

Pete shook his head. 'Too small. The one Rob's got would suit me perfect.'

'Well, he'll be back soon, I shouldn't doubt. You can tackle him then.'

'Yeah, sure,' Pete grunted. 'I'm just a bit anxious to get started, that's all. I hate hangin' about an' watchin' things get worse by the minute.' He sat up straight and shook himself. 'Never mind my dooms an' disasters – how's life with you?'

Den made a so-so waggle with his hand. 'Business is fine. Otherwise – well, let's just say me private life could use livenin' up a bit.'

'I thought it was lively enough already.' Den's long-standing affair with an up-market lady from Knightsbridge was a source of fascination to Pete. He could never understand how a man could live two separate lives and stay intact; yet for Den, it appeared to take no effort at all. 'How many more birds do you want, for heaven's sake?'

Den glanced warily along the bar at Angie. 'The business needs too much of my time,' he murmured. 'I can't get away as often as I'd like. Not even half as often.'

'Well . . .' Pete rubbed his hands. 'Maybe I'll be in that happy position meself, if the old door-to-door takes off.'

'What, gettin' a bit on the side, you mean?'

'No, you berk.' Pete made a face. 'Bein' too busy to catch me breath, that's what I mean.'

Arthur Fowler was weaving his way across the room, clutching a half-empty glass. He stopped beside Pete. 'What're you doin' sittin' at the bar?' he demanded. 'Me an' Pauline an' Mum an' Ethel are sittin' over there. Bring your drink across.'

Pete assessed Arthur's condition at a glance. 'Sorry mate, I didn't see you.' As he stood up from the stool Arthur turned away again. 'Hey, steady

. . .' Pete took his arm. 'I'll come back with you – I don't think you'll make it on your own.' He picked up his drink and winked at Den. 'I best go across an' pay me respects. Remember, if you see Rob Burkett before I do . . .'

'Don't worry,' Den said. 'I'll put him on to you.'

'Ta, mate.' Pete took a firm grip on Arthur's arm and led him back to the table.

Later, when time had been called and customers were leaving the pub in a trickle, Mark Fowler sat on a bench in the garden at the centre of Albert Square. He was staring at the lighted windows of the pub, watching them change size and brightness, seeing the oblongs of yellow turn a shimmering green the longer he stared at them. That was odd, he thought. It was unsettling, too, but Mark didn't think he could look away. He had no idea how long he had been sitting there, his neck fixed and incapable of swivelling his head in another direction.

Although he couldn't see if anyone else was on the bench, he was pretty sure Nick Cotton had gone. For a while they had sat there and talked, but after maybe ten minutes Nick's words had become too strange for Mark to understand. Even his own voice had gone out of control; he'd shaped phrases in his head, but they hadn't come out the way he had planned. Eventually he had gone silent, and so had Nick.

For a long time after that, things around him began to shift subtly; he never actually saw the lamp post opposite move, but it had been a foot or so nearer each time he looked at it. The bushes in the garden changed places. The bench itself had somehow turned, so that it was eventually facing the pub. It was then Mark began staring at the windows, without even needing to blink.

Suddenly he found he could move his head again. He looked down at his hands, ghostly pale in the darkness. They looked enormous. He raised one and touched his face. His fingers felt dampness. He must have been crying, he thought. That didn't seem particularly strange, or important.

He stood up and felt himself sway. He grabbed the back of the bench and clung to it as the ground tilted and tried to shake him off. He imagined himself floating out into endless space if he so much as relaxed his grip. Sudden panic flared and he dropped down on the seat again. He would be safe, he knew, as long as he stayed there.

'Mark? Is that you?'

Two things were happening. A great peace was settling on him, and a woman was coming towards the railings that surrounded the garden.

'Mark?'

It was . . . Who was she? A woman, with a voice he knew, but he couldn't identify her.

'What's up with him, for God's sake?'

There was another woman now. They were coming into the garden. They were standing in front of him.

'Have you been drinkin'?'

It was his mother. Of course it was. And the other one was his Gran. Mark felt great happiness at the sight of them. He smiled, feeling that he could make his mouth as wide as he wanted.

'A right pair, him an' his father,' Lou said. 'Boozin' must run in their blood.'

'Come on,' Pauline said, pulling him to his feet.

He seemed to float upright. 'Hello, Mum.'

'Let's get you home. It's a good job your dad's too legless himself to see the state you're in.'

Mark let the two women lead him across to the house on rubbery, wonderfully relaxed legs. He was high, he thought, this was what high was all about, this was a trip. It was magic. At the gate his mother propped him on the wall while his Gran, muttering, fumbled out her house keys. Mark grinned at them both.

'Silly young devil,' Pauline grunted. 'You're goin' straight to bed, that's where you're goin'.'

Bed would be great, he thought. He would float above it and he would see fabulous pictures in the dark. Nick had been right. Hash was ace. Mark had never felt so terrific in his life. As they began easing him in through the front door, he wondered how much it would cost to get some more.

April

It took three days to get the inside of Rob Burkett's van looking like a greengrocer's. Using wooden struts from old fruit crates and planks liberated from a kerbside skip, Pete made a framework round three sides of the back enclosure and mounted twenty-two boxes, neatly sloped, on the makeshift display stand. He curtained off the space underneath and filled it with sacks of potatoes and the bulkier vegetables. Above the display boxes he hung bright advertising posters scrounged from Covent Garden, and he added a few of his own with bargains listed in multi-coloured lettering executed by young Ian.

'So what do you think?' Pete stood back and folded his arms as he let Kathy see his new business premises for the first time. 'Pretty classy, eh?'

She had to admit it wasn't bad. After years of coping with the restrictions of shape and size on the market barrow, she found the van layout spacious and pleasing to look at.

'All you're goin' to need now is some customers.'

'They'll bowl along, don't you worry.'

'Well . . .' Kathy had a lot of doubts about the venture. Even now, looking at the impressive display, she couldn't muster much hope. 'Folk don't just come runnin' as soon as they see somethin' new. It could take a lot of time.'

Pete dismissed that with a wave. 'What housewife

can resist the convenience of a shop turnin' up right outside her door?'

'A dearer shop than the one on the corner,' Kathy reminded him.

'Right – so they might have to cough up a few more coppers than they'd spend with the bloody consortium. But bein' able to nip out in their slippers an' pinnies to get the fruit an' veg makes it well worthwhile.'

Kathy took his hand and squeezed it. 'I'm not tryin' to put a damper on, love, honest I'm not. But I don't want you to go out there thinkin' it's a piece of cake.'

'I won't do that. But I've got to think positive, haven't I?'

''Course you have.' She kissed his cheek then stood back, drawing her coat about her. 'Come on. Shut up your shop an' come home for your supper. It's well after ten.'

They lived four floors up in the tower block estate behind Albert Square. The flat was cosy and well-furnished, although Pete's niggling urge to keep up with the neighbours tended to show in the over-elaborate decoration and the ostentatious kitchen gadgets. As they came in, Ian was finishing his homework at one end of the dining table. He smiled brightly at them, but Kathy knew straight away something was wrong. She knew it more on instinct than on evidence, and the same instinct told her not to question the boy in front of Pete.

'Still at it, Professor?' Pete ruffled Ian's hair as he unbuttoned his coat. 'You've enough books there to open a library.'

Ian tapped his notepad. 'I've been doin' an essay on the Norman kings.'

Pete sat down at the other end of the table. 'Which ones were they? Henry Fifth, Henry Sixth – that lot?'

Ian did an eye-roll. 'They were the House of Lancaster. I've been writin' about William the Conqueror, William Rufus, Henry the First an' the rest of that bunch.' He stacked the books and stood up. 'Nowadays there's more to school than smokin' in the bogs an' ticklin' little girls behind the bike shed.'

'All right, all right, smart Alec.' Pete rested his elbows on the table and cocked his head at Ian. 'Where's this learnin' gonna get you, anyway? Can you make a livin' out of knowin' all about William the Conqueror?'

'Of course you can,' Ian said. He went to the door, affecting a little swagger. 'But don't worry about it, Dad. When I've got a bagful of degrees an' a job in Whitehall I'll still talk to you. I'm not proud.'

Pete grinned at Kathy as the boy went off to his room. 'He's gettin' right mouthy, isn't he?'

'Just like his old man.' Kathy stepped into the open kitchen area and got Pete's meal out of the oven. 'I sometimes wonder what he *will* do when he leaves school. He's clever an' he's got the gift of the gab – with a bit of the right kind of luck he could go places, couldn't he?'

Pete watched her as she put the plate in front of him. 'Don't go buildin' your hopes too high in that direction, Kath. In my day it was hard enough gettin' a shortcut out of this area. These days it's damn near impossible.' Pete's views on social and political matters were never too distinct, even to himself. A confusion of personal ambitions and built-in prejudices kept him suspended somewhere between capitalist ideals and socialist sentiments. 'Maybe Thatcher'll have stepped down by the time he starts lookin' for a job. But like I said, don't get your hopes up too high.'

'I'm just doin' the same as you,' Kathy said. 'Thinkin' positive, remember?' She wiped her hands on a tea cloth and went to the hallway door. 'I'll just have a word with Ian about helpin' me on the stall at dinner time tomorrow.'

Pete said something through a mouthful of food as she closed the door behind her. She tapped on Ian's door and poked her head in. He was packing his books into a battered school case.

'Got a minute, love?'

He looked at her a little guardedly. 'Yeah, sure.'

Kath came in and sat on the end of the bed. Ian carried on packing the books with his back half turned to her.

Kathy suddenly felt awkward. Increasingly, she realized that when she spoke to Ian she was no longer addressing a child. He had to be approached with the same consideration and restraint an adult would expect. He couldn't simply be talked down to.

'I was wonderin' if you'd help out on the stall tomorrow.' It was an opening, although it was hardly the point of her coming to his room. 'It'd let me get one or two things done in the dinner hour.'

'Sure.' Ian snapped the case shut and turned to

70

her. 'How long are you goin' to look after the stall on your own, anyway?'

'As long as I have to. Until your Dad's made a decent go of the van round. We don't want to give up the stall just yet. I mean it'd be puttin' all our eggs in one basket, wouldn't it?'

Ian sat down on his bedside stool. For someone so young, he could look extraordinarily serious. He was doing it now, fixing his mother with steady, probing eyes. 'Tell me honestly, Mum. Do you think Dad's got any chance of makin' it with his van?'

'He's got as much chance as anybody . . .'

'That's not what I asked you.'

'Well, he wouldn't try if he didn't think – '

'Oh come on, Mum. It's a real desperation job, isn't it? He's in deep trouble, double deep, or he wouldn't even dream of goin' round the streets tryin' to flog his stuff. It ain't his style.'

Kathy looked at those steady eyes, the firm conviction in the angle of his jaw. It was no part of being a mother to let your child feel insecure, she often reminded herself of that. She had always wanted to shield Ian from domestic anxieties, because she still remembered, vividly, how that kind of worry had eaten at her when she was a girl. But how could she protect an inquisitive, intelligent boy who could sense some things so easily?

'Is that what was wrong when we came in, Ian? You brightened up a bit too sharpish. Somethin' was botherin' you. Had you been sittin' through there worryin' about the business?'

'Sort of.' He shifted on the stool, his eyes averted

now. 'I'd been worryin', all right – about a bloke that came to the door while you were out.'

Kathy felt a small pang of fright. 'A bloke? What bloke?' Her thoughts raced. A man at the door, her son in the flat alone. There were so many stories about terrible things happening. 'Who was he?'

'His name's Gower. When I told him you weren't in I don't think he believed me, at first. He looked pretty mad. He said you'd know what he'd come about an' I'd to tell you he'd be back.'

Kathy nodded. Relief and a renewal of worry collided in her, making her feel queasy. 'That's all right, love,' she murmured. 'It's somethin' that'll get sorted out.'

'What was he, Mum? Some kind of collector?'

She nodded. 'Somethin' like that.'

Gower was the local agent of a firm that issued credit cheques. They could be used at various shops to buy clothing and other goods. Ian's winter outfit, his school uniform and football boots had been bought with two of the cheques. No repayments had been made for three weeks and Kathy had ignored the warning letters, hoping something would turn up. Gower had been to the door once already and she had promised him settlement of the arrears in a week's time. That had been ten days ago.

'Look, Ian, I want you to know somethin'. Whatever happens, however bad things get, you'll be all right. The lot of us'll be all right. You've got to believe that an' stop worryin'.'

'But what if Dad goes bust?'

'He won't. Your Dad's a shrewd enough cookie to keep his head above water.'

'But he's bein' squeezed out of business, isn't he?'

'Ian, I told you. You can rely on him. He won't let anythin' bad happen.' To make him feel safe was paramount. No child of hers would go through the misery she had suffered – the terrible atmosphere in the house, the fear of every knock at the door, her mother crying in the night. 'We'll not be destitute or out on the street or anythin' like that.'

Ian stared at the floor for a moment, then he stood up and began unbuttoning his shirt. 'I'd best be gettin' to bed,' he said.

'Promise me you'll stop frettin', will you?'

Without looking at her he said, 'I promise I'll try.'

When Kathy went back to the lounge Pete had already cleared his plate and was rinsing it at the sink.

'That was lovely, Kath. I ate every scrap an' a bit off the pattern on the plate.'

Kathy went and stood beside him, holding the tea towel ready. 'Big day tomorrow, eh?'

'Yup.' Pete handed her the plate. 'I can hardly wait.'

'Neither can I.' She hoped it didn't sound too hollow. When the plate, knife and fork were dried she put them away. 'Fancy watchin' a bit of telly, Pete?'

'I thought I'd have an early night.'

'Oh.' She considered that. 'Well, if you don't mind, I think I'll just watch a bit of the film.'

'Do what you want, love.' Pete drew her close for a moment and kissed her. 'Just don't sit up too late. We've got a hard day ahead of us tomorrow.'

When he had gone to bed Kathy switched on the television and sat down. On ITV a man was talking about the Queen Mother opening a new paddock complex at Kempton Park. Kathy hit the remote control and got a woman this time. She was discussing the executions in Florida and Louisiana of a child-killer and a double murderer. A tap on another button brought on the film. Peter Cushing was reacting with shock at the disappearance of four vital compounds from his laboratory.

Kath sat back, staring at the screen, not even trying to comprehend the action. The point of this exercise was to weary herself to a point where she would fall asleep as soon as she got into bed. Otherwise she would lie awake and go over the formula for disaster that had become the reality of their daily lives. Their money was all gone. They would soon have no credit to draw on with the wholesalers. They were in debt in too many places. And their prospects were poor. Kathy ran it all through her head again, like a prospector panning mud with the hope of finding just a glimmer of gold.

On the screen a character in a tall hat turned to camera and said, 'This is terrible! Terrible!'

Kathy nodded wearily, yawned and sank a little deeper into the chair.

On the morning of the sixteenth, Lofty got to the offices of B. French Enterprises in a more distracted state of mind than usual. The night before, the comedian Tommy Cooper had died. Tommy had been one of Lofty's favourites. Apart from being funny, the man had always struck a chord of familiarity in Lofty; there was something about the feckless style he adopted on stage, the dithering and, above all, the thorough lack of malice that had made him an avuncular soul-mate. Lofty hadn't been able to get Tommy Cooper out of his head all morning. He felt he had lost a good friend.

Today the office door was opened by a man he had never seen before. He was tall, hook-nosed and pasty looking, like someone who spent very little time in the daylight.

'Yes?' he enquired. 'Can I help you?'

'Um, yeah . . .' Lofty made tight juggling movements with his hands. 'I'm, ah, I'm Lofty.'

The man's mouth hardened into a thin line for a moment. 'So?'

'I've come for the boxes.'

'Really.' The man stepped back, ushering him in. His eyes had lost their flat look. 'Sit down, will you?'

There were two other men in the room. One was a stranger, the other was Barry French. The stranger was standing and Barry was sitting stiffly at the desk where the girl usually sat. He was trying not to look troubled.

'So you're Lofty,' the tall one said, 'and you've come for the boxes.'

'That's right.' Lofty sat down and glanced at Barry again. He was running a hand through his hair and attempting to out-stare something invisible on the desk.

'I'm here about the boxes, too,' the big man said. 'I'm Denis, by the way. Denis Cuffey.'

Lofty gave him a cordial little nod. 'Pleased to meet you, Denis.'

'I'd prefer it if you called me Mr Cuffey, actually. Or Inspector.' He pointed to the other man. 'He's John Wallace. If he speaks to you, call him Mr Wallace, or Sergeant.'

Lofty pushed up his glasses. He had a feeling he was going to find out more about the job he had been doing.

'What were you planning to do with the boxes, Lofty?'

'Erm, well . . .'

'You must know.' Cuffy came closer, bending slightly and examining Lofty's face, the way a doctor might. 'No use dreaming up any corny stories. We'll find out the truth soon enough.'

This was beginning to feel very serious. Lofty swallowed hard and jiggled his hands again. 'I was goin' to put them on the van an' deliver them,' he said.

'Where?'

'To the addresses on the slips.'

'What slips?'

Lofty gulped. 'The slips they put on the boxes.'

Cuffey turned and glared at Barry French. 'Where are these slips?'

Barry's face went innocent with incredible speed. 'What slips? I don't know what he's talking about. I don't even know who he is, for that matter.'

Cuffy groaned softly. 'Barry, your next good lie will be your first one. I'll ask you again – where are the slips, the delivery details for those boxes?'

'I haven't got any.'

'And you don't know how the boxes got here, the piles of them down there in the old garage and the stack through there in the other office.'

Barry shrugged, a helpless victim of circumstance. 'That's what I said, and it's the truth.'

The Inspector took out a cigarette packet, put one in his mouth and lit it. He stood there puffing smoke into the space between himself and Barry, letting the tension build. 'You're a lying bag of shit,' he said finally. 'Sergeant Wallace, I think we should separate these two, before Mr French sets up an eyeball tic-tac with his minion here.'

Lofty was stunned. Once, when he had been in the army, the Military Police questioned him about the theft of a radio. He had known everybody was being questioned anyway, but it made no difference. They had terrified him, the way they kept even the immediate future from him, not giving him a clue what would happen next. It was like walking in a dark, unfamiliar room with gaping holes in the floor.

'Come on, son.'

Lofty took a moment to react, then he realized the Sergeant wanted to take him into the other room. He stood up, glancing at Barry again. The man looked as apprehensive as Lofty felt. At least, though, Barry knew what it was all about.

'Take the chair in front of the desk,' Wallace said as he closed the office door. To Lofty, he didn't look nearly so formidable as Cuffey, but there was no way of telling with policemen.

'It's a bit of a do, this. Isn't it?'

Lofty didn't feel qualified to answer. He blinked

at Wallace as he strolled to the corner and lightly kicked one of the white cartons.

'I suppose you know the penalties?'

Lofty wanted to say he didn't even know the crime, but his mouth was drying.

'I'd say, with his record, that Frenchie would pull three to five. As for you . . .'

'But I don't – ' Lofty had to stop suddenly and gulp. 'I'm not anythin' to do with it.'

'To do with what?'

'Whatever it is.'

'Oh come on now, son. You're not going to sit there and tell me you don't know what's going on?'

'But I don't.' Lofty was trembling now. He felt he was being drawn deeper and deeper into a whirlpool. 'I don't even know what's in them boxes.'

Sergeant Wallace lifted the flap of the topmost carton, which had been torn open. He took out one of the dark oblong objects Lofty had been wondering about. Now, seeing it in clear daylight, he found nothing mysterious about it at all. It was a video cassette.

'You work for Barry French,' Wallace said slowly, waving the tape from side to side as if he wanted to mesmerize Lofty with it. 'You come and go with this merchandise. Yet you say you don't know what it is?'

'That's right.'

'But you can see now what it is.'

Lofty nodded.

'They're not blanks, son.'

Expecting to hear more, Lofty looked intently at Wallace. Then he realized he had been left on a dark precipice again. He was being required to wonder, to fret. What were they, then? A strong possible answer flashed into his mind. He had seen videos being handed back and forth at tables in The Vic. They were usually porno. Porno was something Lofty hated, he had seen it only once and he would never watch again. It wasn't just illegal, it was a brutal, ugly violation of something private, a vulgarizing of women who had somehow looked more like meat than living beings. The horror of what he was being linked to hit him like a fist blow.

'But I wouldn't have anythin' to do with that stuff! Not if I knew!'

'What stuff?' Wallace's voice was like the deadly purr of a cat that had just ambushed a mouse. 'How come you know what's on the tapes? I didn't tell you.'

Now Lofty was as indignant as he was scared. What kind of person did they think he was? As he stared at the Sergeant he began to pant. His chest was growing painfully tight. 'I'm telling you – I wouldn't go near anythin' like that! It's disgustin' filth!'

Wallace suddenly looked bewildered. 'What're you on about?'

'That muck in the boxes! All I did was deliver for them – I was never told what it was an' I never took a look. That's the truth, I swear it!'

'Steady, steady.' Wallace dropped the cassette into the box and came across the room. 'Don't get yourself in such a state, for God's sake.' He was peering at Lofty's lips, which were turning blue. 'Have you got something up with your heart?'

Lofty fumbled in his pocket. 'I need me inhaler,' he panted. It wasn't where it usually was. He began to panic as he remembered putting in on the mantelpiece before he came out. He had been so preoccupied, thinking about poor old Tommy Cooper. 'Oh God I've left it.' He had been told not to panic because it made the attacks worse, but he couldn't help himself. He shot to his feet, gasping now, the blueness spreading to his cheeks as a spasm constricted his chest.

'Sit down,' Wallace told him. 'Let me get your shirt unbuttoned.'

'That won't help,' Lofty croaked. 'I need the inhaler.'

Wallace took another look at him then hurried to the door. He yanked it open and called to the Inspector. Culley warned Barry French to stay where he was then came bustling in. He took one look at Lofty then gaped wide-eyed at the Sergeant.

'What the bloody hell's happened?'

'He's got asthma, I think. The attack just came on suddenly. No warning, as far as I could see.'

Culley was at the desk before Wallace finished speaking. He snatched up the telephone and rapidly dialled three nines without looking. His eyes were fixed on Lofty's blue, gasping, half-conscious face.

Lou Beale had her third cup of tea at ten o'clock. She took it to the table in the living room and sat down to look through the paper again. She occasionally wondered why she put herself to the misery of reading the news every day. There was so much misery in the world and little enough room for happiness, yet she could never resist the grim daily sifting of conflict, crime, disaster and death.

Today she found it hard to concentrate on what she read. Her mind kept wandering from Pete to Arthur and back again. So far, Arthur had applied for five jobs, without success. He was off to yet another interview that morning. Pete had been trading from the van for over a week and although there were signs that his venture was working, he was having to struggle. The overall cause for Lou's worry was that both men, in their separate ways, were having to cope with the thin edge of despair. It was there, even though they put up bright facades. Arthur, still a young man, now lived with the knowledge that he was too old for most jobs. Pete, working from early morning until late at night, still wasn't earning half the money he needed to survive, let alone show a profit.

Halfway through a news story about a mugging in North London, Lou pushed the paper away from her. She looked at the clock and wondered if she should go across to the launderette and keep Pauline company. She smiled tightly to herself; the truth was, she was the one who needed company. She stood up and was halfway to the kitchen when the back door opened. It was Arthur.

'How did it go?' she asked him.

'I'll say one thing for all these interviews I'm havin' . . .' He took off his cap and jacket and hung them on the door. 'They're consistent.'

'So you didn't get the job.'

'Right first time.'

Lou watched him fill the kettle and put it on the

cooker. 'There's bound to be somethin' for you, if you keep tryin'.' She suspected the opposite. For a lot of men nowadays it was just the way it had been in the thirties. Employers could have their pick from the glut of young people. To take on anyone over the age of thirty-five was virtually an act of charity.

'Don't worry,' Arthur said, 'I'll keep tryin'.' He turned to Lou. 'Do you know what the bloke told me? He'll be interviewin' for three days – an' it's for an unskilled labourin' job, mind you. His desk's piled up with applications.'

'What reason did he have for turnin' you down?'

'The usual. My age.'

'Ridiculous,' Lou grunted. 'You're as fit as any other man.'

'That cuts no ice, Mum. My birth certificate's like a flamin' death warrant.' He turned and stared at the kettle again. 'But like I said, I'll keep tryin'. It's a terrible feelin' though, knowin' you're handicapped, seein' them gettin' ready to turn you down as soon as they lay eyes on you.'

'Where there's a will there's a way,' Lou said. She was running out of platitudes to hand Arthur, and she was pretty sure they did no good. But what else could she say, or do? She looked at her coat over the chair, feeling guilty about going out now and leaving him. 'I was just thinkin' about goin' over an' seein' Pauline.'

'You do that. It'll cheer her up.'

Lou picked up her coat and put it on. 'Just so long as you don't mind bein' left here on your todd.'

'Nah.' He started to rinse the teapot. 'I'm no kind of company these days, anyway.'

'Right you are, then.'

Lou pulled on her gloves, thinking how her feelings towards Arthur had changed. Her convictions about his laziness had evaporated. She believed that what he had been doing since he lost his job was harder, in its way, than work. He was fighting to keep his dignity. He rose at six every day, washed and shaved and turned himself out smartly. He got on the streets by nine most mornings and trudged around Walford for hours, hunting out job prospects. He never went into pubs, however strong the temptation. Blind alleys were accepted stoically and he always affected a cheerful, optimistic attitude when he was with his wife and children. Lou felt remorse for some of the things she had said about him. His tenacity, in the face of so little hope, was worthy of her Albert – although she would never tell him that.

Ten minutes after Lou had gone out there was a sharp, almost impatient knocking at the front door. Arthur put down the boot he had been polishing and answered it.

'Arthur, can I speak to you for a minute?' It was Dr Legg.

'Yeah, of course. Come in.'

They went through to the living room. Arthur asked if the doctor would like a cup of tea, but he declined. 'I've some calls to make and I'm running a shade late already. But I thought I should talk to you as soon as I could.'

'What's the trouble?'

'I've been having a talk with Pauline . . .'

Arthur looked instantly alarmed. 'What's happened?'

'Don't go upsetting yourself,' Legg said, patting Arthur's shoulder. 'It's just that she came to see me this morning – '

'She didn't tell me there was anythin' up,' Arthur interrupted. 'I don't think she told anybody.'

'Just bear with me for a minute. Sit down.' Legg waited until Arthur had composed himself a little. 'I'm not allowed to go into the details of what's said to me in the surgery, you know that – but in this instance, I think you can be of most help, so I'm bending the rules just a tiny bit.'

'Is Pauline ill, or what?'

'She's not ill, no. In fact it wasn't herself she came to see me about. It was Mark. She's worried about him.'

Arthur thought for a moment. As far as he could recall, the boy had been his normal, surly self lately. 'What does she reckon's wrong, then?'

'It's his behaviour, especially in the mornings before he goes to school. For a time Pauline's been worried that he was drinking. Now she thinks it might be drugs.'

'Has she tackled him about it?'

The doctor shook his head. 'She believed that might only drive things further underground, make him more secretive, more cautious.'

'My God,' Arthur groaned. 'Drugs.'

'We don't know if that's so, of course, but the symptoms Pauline described to me had a familiar ring. I thought you could find out a bit more.'

'How?'

Legg hesitated for a moment, then sighed. 'It's my own observation that Mark's been keeping rather unsound company. There are quite a few tearaways and villains about Walford, but Nick Cotton's a lot more sinister than most.'

'I've warned Mark to have nothin' to do with him . . .'

'What we tell children to do and what they actually do are often poles apart, Arthur. I've seen Mark and Nick together a time or two lately.'

'Right.' Arthur slapped the arm of the chair. 'We'll soon hit that on the head.'

'You'll have to be subtle about it,' Legg pointed out. 'If Mark is into some kind of drug abuse he'll need help. Part of that help would be to get his source of supply cut off. You'd have to find out where he gets it from.'

'Bloody Nick Cotton.'

'It might be Cotton, it might not. There may be no actual problem at all, but we'll only know that from careful investigation.'

'Shouldn't I tackle Mark with it, right out in the open?'

'No, I don't think so,' Legg said. 'I think Pauline was right not to say anything to him.'

'How come?'

'Because drug users become the most secretive and devious people around, once they think somebody's on to them.'

Arthur thought about that, then he nodded. 'I can see the point, I suppose. I wish she'd said somethin' to me about it, though.'

'She didn't want to worry you – you've got enough

troubles as it is. But in my view, you're the very man to get a stop put to this. But be careful, we don't want to go following any false trails. We don't want to blow a nothing up into something, either.' Legg looked at his watch. 'I've got to run, Arthur.' He started buttoning his coat.

'What do you reckon I should actually do?' Arthur asked him.

'Observation's the best procedure, for now. Try to watch the boy's movements, without letting him know. If you do find there's a supplier, I'm sure you've enough instinct to know how to handle that. And if Mark does have a habit, the rest will be up to me.'

At the door, Dr Legg cautioned Arthur not to say anything to Pauline. 'It might all seem a bit underhanded, but we have to be practical. I've told her I'd speak to somebody who could handle the problem without involving the authorities. There's no need to tell her it's you – not for the moment, anyway. That way things'll look a lot more natural all round.'

When the doctor had gone Arthur stood in the kitchen, staring out at the yard. It was amazing how one problem could make another one seem insignificant. Until that knock at the door he had been exclusively concerned with his own dismal situation. Now, landed with the possibility that his son was taking drugs, his jobless condition hardly seemed to matter. He thought of Pauline, keeping her apprehension from him, protecting him from more distress.

'Poor darlin',' he murmured.

Maybe this was what life was all about, he thought. Life for the Fowlers, anyway; not many high spots, not many laughs, just lots of occasions when a new problem would crop up to give them a break from an old one.

'You had us worried for a while there,' Sergeant Wallace told Lofty.

'I was pretty worried meself.'

They were in a cubicle at the King George VI Hospital's Casualty Department. Lofty was propped up on the bed, fully clothed, with a blanket draped over him. He had been there for an hour and was waiting for clearance to go home.

'The oxygen they gave me in the ambulance was a blessin',' he said. 'An' that jab was magic. My chest just sort of cleared, like that.' He tried to snap his fingers, but failed.

'Anyway,' Wallace said, 'if it's any consolation, the Inspector's decided not to take any proceedings against you.'

Lofty blinked at him. 'Do you reckon he'd have done the same if I hadn't had that attack?'

'Oh, I think the truth would have emerged. Your attack just sort of speeded up the process of investigation.'

'How come?'

'Well, you obviously didn't know a thing about what was going on. You were a delivery boy, that's all. Strictly speaking, we should have you up in court, where they'd only acquit you anyway. This way we take the tension out of it, eh?'

Lofty nodded. 'Thanks a lot.' The injection had

left him disorientated. That, plus the mystery still surrounding the morning's other events, made him feel as if he was inhabiting somebody else's life. 'What made you think I'd nothin' to do with what was goin' on?'

'The way you jumped the gun about the porno. It *was* porno you were on about, wasn't it?'

'Yeah.'

'Well, Barry French hasn't been dabbling in naughty movies, Lofty.'

'What are they, then?'

'Pirates. Copies of legitimate commercial cassettes. We got on to them about two weeks ago. They're good pirates, made on very professional equipment, and the distribution was pretty cute. There must have been four or five drop-off points before any of them reached their final destinations.' He rubbed his hands, like a chef who'd finally made a recipe work. 'We've got it stitched up now, or most of it. All you have to do is let us have the names and addresses you remember and we can be pretty sure we've wiped out French's racket.'

'Yeah, sure.' Lofty watched the policeman get out his notebook. He knew this was the right thing to do. He was helping to punish a bunch of villains. Even so, it felt like a betrayal. As he began to rhyme off the names he could recall, he secretly hoped that at least some of them, if they truly weren't very bad men, would slip the net.

Five minutes later a nurse came and told Lofty his blood serum had been checked and he was free to go home. With a new inhaler in his pocket he got into the police car with Sergeant Wallace, who drove him across Walford to the end of Bridge Street and let him out.

'Thanks again for your help,' Wallace called as he drove off.

'Yeah. That's all right.' Lofty looked about him to make sure nobody had heard. The last thing he needed was for people to think he was a grass.

As he strolled along under the railway bridge he glanced across at Ali's and decided he could use a cup of tea. When he got inside Sue was giving Ali a muted chewing as he worked at the hotplate.

'I'm havin' new furniture,' she hissed as Lofty stepped up to the counter. '*New*, get it? It's bad enough I'm goin' to have to live in that – that hole, without you tryin' to gob me off with a load of your dad's old chairs an' his busted sofa.' She turned sharply to Lofty. 'Yes?' she demanded.

'Cup of tea please, Sue. An' could I have a fried egg an' a deep slice?'

She nodded curtly and poured the tea. As Lofty wandered away with it she turned on Ali again. 'Your attitude really floors me, do you know that? One minute you're sayin' only the best's good enough for me, then next thing you're treatin' me like Second-Hand Rose.'

'I'm only tryin' to economize,' Ali complained. 'It's costin' me plenty to get the place decorated, remember.'

Sue stepped back a pace, hands on hips, eyebrows high. 'What? You've got to be jokin'. Eight rolls of paper you could spit peas through and some rusty cans of paint off the market – you call that pricey? Nobody could have done it cheaper. Nobody.'

'I've got to pay a bloke to do it, remember.'

'Yeah, an' most likely it'll be some dosser without a straight eye in his head that'll do it for a fiver plus the price of a bottle of meths.'

'He's a qualified decorator,' Ali said indignantly. 'He's the best.'

'I'm just sick of the whole business – the flat, the drudgery, *me*.' Sue glanced down at herself. 'Look at me, I'm about the size of a whale. Seven months gone an' I look more like ten.' The observation put her back on the original tack. 'Two months away from havin' a baby, I am. Two months, an' I'm expected to go through all this hassle over gettin' settled into a God-awful house any decent person wouldn't be caught dead in.'

Ali turned from the hotplate. 'Take it easy, Sue. You're gettin' hysterical. You know what they told you at the clinic about your blood pressure.'

'Sod my bleedin' blood pressure.' She stepped through to the back and got her coat. 'I'm goin' out for a bit. See to Lofty's egg an' deep slice, will you?'

'Where are you goin'?'

'Up on to the bridge,' she snapped, heading for the door. 'To put meself under a train.'

Since he had sat down, Lofty had been having his own ears assaulted by Dot Cotton, who had moved up two tables to get closer to him, after he had deliberately taken a seat as far from her as he could.

'I can tell there's no harmony between them two,' Dot muttered as Sue went out. 'I'm not a person who believes in racial prejudice mind you, but it stands to reason. It's hard enough as it is for man

90

an' wife to get on, without introducin' difficulties like that.' She waggled her head as her eyes darted around the place, making a random inventory. 'I mean, he'd be better off with one of his own kind, wouldn't he? There'd be more natural harmony.'

'Yeah,' Lofty said, wishing he hadn't ordered the food. That way he could have gulped down the tea and left.

Dot went silent for the length of time it took to light a cigarette. 'Not workin' today, then?' she enquired, blowing smoke in a wreath around Lofty's head.

'Um, no. I'd one of me asthma attacks. Thought I'd best take it easy.'

'It's a dangerous thing, asthma.' Dot patted her own rickety chest. 'I've had the odd brush with it meself – although I think I tend more towards emphysema. It's odd, me havin' such a delicate constitution an' yet my boy's such a robust, healthy individual.'

Lofty had been wondering about her boy. For one thing, he wanted to thank him for getting him the job with Barry French. 'Is Nick about this mornin', Dot?'

She shrugged. 'He can be a dark one, Lofty. After his breakfast he just said he'd see me later, no explanations or nothin'. I've always said he would be suited for diplomacy or somethin' like that. He's good at keepin' himself a closed book.'

'Yeah, I've noticed that.'

Mercifully, Dot realized suddenly that she was late for her appointment with the optician. 'The last one told me there's nothin' wrong with me eyes, but he wasn't on this side of them. There's somethin' wrong, all right.' She rose and gathered her bag and gloves, simultaneously scattering ash across the table. 'I'll see you around then, Lofty. Take care now.'

As she moved off Ali brought the egg and fried bread. He seemed much brighter now that Sue had gone. 'What kind of day are you havin' so far, Lofty?'

'Oh, so-so.' He didn't feel like going into any of it. 'How about you?'

'Well.' Ali held up his hand and ticked off the events on his fingers. 'I broke three bottles of milk, got hot fat all over me shoes, charged somebody too much for his soup an' got a long-runnin' bollockin' off the wife. Pretty standard mornin', really. Oh yeah, an' I got offered a part-time job I couldn't take, because of the hours.'

'What kind of job?'

'Drivin',' Ali said. 'The sort of thing that'd be up your street, as a matter of fact. But you've got a job, haven't you?'

Lofty shook his head. 'It fell through on me.'

'Hang on.' Ali went behind the counter and fumbled about among some receipt books. 'Ah, got it.' He came back with a slip of paper. 'That's the number, if you want to ring the guy. He's an old mate of mine from the mini-cab days. Bell him any time after two, an' say I recommended you. You never know your luck, he might take you on.'

'That's great, Ali.' After such a traumatic start, the day was beginning to look promising after all.

He pocketed the paper, picked up his knife and fork and began attacking the food.

Across the road in the launderette, Pauline Fowler was coming to the end of her early shift. She had already mopped the floor and wiped down the tops of the machines. She was stacking the bags of service washes as Arthur came in. She looked up and smiled cheerfully. Too cheerfully, he thought.

'I thought I'd stick me head in an' tell you I didn't get that labourin' job,' he said. 'Better you know it before you get home.'

'Mum told me already,' Pauline said. 'It hasn't got you down too much, has it?'

'Of course it hasn't.' He dipped into his pocket and held up a folded sheet of paper. 'I've just got meself another three possibles. Den came across from the pub with them. He'd been earwiggin' the draymen's gossip while they were deliverin' his bitter.'

'Aw, isn't that good of him?'

'Yeah. It's nice to know how many mates you've got.' Arthur turned and looked around the place. 'Anythin' I can do to help?'

'No, love, it's nearly all done.' Pauline was about to explain that the new woman would be there in a few minutes when the door opened and Nick Cotton came in. Pauline saw the instantaneous change in Arthur.

'Mum's not been in, has she?' Nick asked.

'No, I haven't seen her today,' Pauline said. She looked at Arthur again. He was glaring at Nick, his jaw working tensely.

'All right, Arthur?'

'I'm fine Nick.' It sounded like a threat in code. Arthur turned away suddenly, his head bowed.

'Well, I'll be seein' you, then.' Nick threw one sharp inquisitive look at Pauline, then left.

'Arthur. What is it?'

He looked at her. 'What?'

'You looked at him like you wanted to pull his ears off.'

Arthur took a deep breath. 'It's nothin', love.'

'Are you sure?'

He nodded. The sudden appearance of Nick Cotton had thrown him off balance. He had spent the best part of an hour thinking what he would do if he found out that man was supplying his son with drugs. In that space of time Arthur's thoughts had turned very dark. Only the arrival of Den had shaken him out of it.

'It's nothin' at all, love,' he told Pauline, squeezing her elbow. He would have to learn to hide his feelings around Nick Cotton. No good end would be served if he flew off the handle prematurely. He could even do Mark a lot of harm. But if he did discover there was foul work afoot, he knew exactly what he wanted to do to Mr Cotton – what he *would* do, given cause. It was the kind of thing he would call mindless violence, if anybody else did it.

June

As the year moved sluggishly into summer, events at large gave sure signs that 1984 was to be no different from any other recent years. It would certainly be no better. In London the House of Commons had a marathon sitting to discuss a Government Bill to abolish the Greater London Council. At about the same time the Foreign Office expelled a man they described as the KGB controller in London, while elsewhere it was announced, as unemployment remained above the three-million mark, that salary increases of up to 18 per cent had been approved for State Industry chairmen. There was a cheerless familiarity to all this news, as if life was cunningly moving in a circle.

Even accidents and disasters had recognizable profiles. Four British people were killed in an avalanche near Zermatt; in the Falklands eight people died in a hospital fire; eight British holidaymakers were killed when a coach crashed on the island of Majorca. Further afield it was announced that a huge explosion at a Soviet naval arsenal had obliterated many surface-to-air missiles and killed an unknown number of people. It was business as usual worldwide, with even the nuclear threat no more of a menace than it had been a year or even two years ago. Whatever way the historians chose to depict

1984, it wouldn't be recorded in any of the books as an exceptional year.

For the inhabitants of Albert Square the days passed as ordinarily as they did anywhere else. At the beginning of June, Arthur Fowler was still without a job. He hadn't found any evidence, either, of his son's possible flirtation with drugs. His mother-in-law continued to suffer the occasional chest pains, although recently they had been milder. Pete Beale was struggling along, scraping a living off his van-round and his stall, finding it a little harder each week to make ends meet. Lofty Holloway was working part-time transporting foodstuffs from a warehouse to various restaurants, and he was still putting in his three nights a week at The Vic. Sue and Ali Osman, now living at number 23, were preparing for the arrival of their baby. Den Watts was still having an affair and Angie still lived on her nerves. Life went on. Nobody expected miracles.

Lofty Holloway was perhaps an exception. He was growing very interested in a form of miracle-working known as PL, which was short for Persuasive Light. Prior to discovering PL, he had decided that if he was ever to make anything of himself, he would have to project his personality with some force. It wasn't an idea he took to easily – staying on life's sidelines suited him best, but that was getting him nowhere. It had seemed like a sign, therefore, when he found Dr Rami Shah's book, *Personal Enhancement Through Persuasive Light*, going for fifteen pence on the second-hand book barrow on the market.

'The idea's beautifully straightforward,' he told

Angie one slow Friday night in the pub when she had the patience to listen to him. 'You just do a simple exercise three times a day, an' at the end of a month you find you're havin' lots more influence over people.'

Angie pursed her shiny lips for a moment. 'Influence over them? You mean like a hypnotist?'

'No, not like that – what I mean is you're more impressive, you can persuade them to do things . . .'

'Sounds a bit dodgy to me, Lofty. You be careful you don't get yourself in bother.' Although her commonest response to Lofty was impatience with his perpetual faffing about, she felt a deeper, affectionate protectiveness towards him, too. 'You know what happened to them Americans that got it in their heads they was super-bein's. They started holdin' up banks an' jumpin' off the tops of buildin's an' God knows what.'

Lofty wished he could make it clearer. 'It's this light everybody's got at their centre, Angie. It's a mixture of character, spirit, knowledge – the best features of all them things. The exercises concentrate it an' make it more powerful. You're able to affect people in a positive way . . .' He tailed off, seeing she still didn't get it. It was so simple, really. Shining your personality light was what it was all about. Casting your positive beam, opening up opportunities because important people could see the value in you.

'Why don't you take up somethin' really useful?' Angie suggested. 'Don't tamper with your head so much. Get a hobby.'

'But I want to get on before I take up hobbies. I

mean, hobbies are for your spare time, they're somethin' to relax with when you're not workin'. I've more spare time than work time. I'll get a hobby or two when my spare time's a bit more precious.'

Angie shrugged. 'Go ahead, then. Get your internal light burnin' full pelt an' see where it all ends up.' She giggled. 'You'll most likely get done for flashin'.'

Lofty resented her making jokes about things he took seriously. 'I'm only tryin' to better meself,' he pointed out. 'PL sounds as likely a way as any, for the likes of me.'

Angie realized she was hurting his feelings. 'Whatever you say, love.' She looked around the half empty bar. Even Den was leaning on the corner, yawning. 'Tell you what. Have yourself a break while things are sluggish. Practise your exercises or somethin', eh?'

Lofty thanked her, got the book from his coat pocket and took it with him to a vacant table. He sat down, unfolded the corner of the page he had been reading and peered at the small type. After a minute he sat back to have a think. As he saw it, Dr Shah was saying that people were giving off personality light all the time; the problem was that not a lot of them ever knew how to make it even a little bit persuasive – it was, in the doctor's phrase, 'usually too diffuse to do more than glimmer'. It followed, therefore, that the man who knew how to concentrate his light was the one who held most of the cards. It was a staggering thought. Right there in his hands Lofty had the power to manipulate life, to shape his own destiny.

He made sure no one was looking, then he closed the book and got ready to perform the exercise that would intensify his light. All he had to do was stare at a point on the wall – Lofty chose a beer stain beside the juke box – and imagine rays of light from his brain, his bowels and his heart coming together at a point behind his eyes. The bit about his bowels troubled him slightly, but he was sure Dr Shah knew what he was talking about.

After a minute he could feel it working. There was definitely a sensation of terrific inner brightness. He imagined the golden beams overlapping at the backs of his eyes, making a glow as fierce as a roman candle. It was so intense he could feel the heat. The brilliance of it made his spirit rise. He could imagine himself being confident, potent, ready to bestride the world.

'What's up with you?' Den demanded. 'You look constipated.'

Lofty jumped. 'God, Den, you didn't half give me a start.'

Den was leaning across the bar. 'Who said anythin' to you about dreamin' on the job? I've got a couple of customers waitin' to be served.'

'Sorry.' Lofty snatched up his book and got to his feet. 'Angie said I could take five minutes . . .'

'I'm the boss,' Den said briskly. 'She's the boss's missus, which ain't the same thing at all. Bear that in mind, will you?'

'Sure.' Lofty nodded over-vigorously. His head

felt funny now the light had been so abruptly dimmed. 'I'll remember, Den.'

'Come on then, chop chop.'

Lofty got behind the bar. It was Debbie and Andy who were waiting. Andy asked for their usual pint and a half. As Lofty was pulling the drinks he suddenly realized he had been thrown into the path of an opportunity. He needed practice with his PL, so who better to try it on than Debbie?

He took a minute to consider it carefully. Of all the people who came into the pub, Debbie Wilkins was the one who made the greatest impression on him. He wouldn't go so far as to say he fancied her; it was all wrong to fancy another man's woman. On the other hand, he had to admit that his admiration stopped just short of infatuation. In his subdued way he had always played up to Debbie, yet he knew she hardly ever noticed him. The flaw, clearly, had been the absence of Persuasive Light. So why not try it on her and see if it made any change in her attitude to him? If she even began noticing him more it would be a bonus.

'One pint and one half,' he said, bringing the drinks to where the couple were sitting. He took the money and thought over the little ploy once again as he got their change from the till. He decided there was nothing to lose by trying – and the way the glow had swelled in him a couple of minutes ago, he reckoned there was a lot to be gained.

Another ten minutes passed before he could try anything. People had started coming into the pub in small crowds. Lofty worked at double speed, which impressed Angie more than any amount of PL ever could. When the backlog of punters had been cleared he stood by the door to the back for a moment, catching his breath and developing his composure. All he had to do was imagine the light beaming forth. The rest would be automatic.

He turned and sauntered along the bar, remembering to push his specs well up along his nose. He stopped beside Debbie and Andy.

'You two keepin' busy, then?'

They had been talking intently to one another when Lofty butted in. They both stopped and looked at him.

'Busy, are you?' Lofty said again. It was quite hard to talk and imagine the light at the same time, but he believed he could manage it.

Andy frowned. 'What – at work, d'you mean?'

Lofty nodded, aiming his light right at Debbie.

'Yes,' Andy said, 'I suppose I'm pretty busy. Nursing's always a busy game. Illness never takes a holiday.' He appeared to hope that would do the trick and get Lofty on the move again. But it didn't. He stayed where he was, leaning casually on the bar, his eyes trained on Debbie.

'And you, Debs? Are you busy?'

She smiled politely. 'Yes, thank you.'

'I suppose bankin's pretty tough.' He watched her carefully. Something was happening already. Instead of the usual offhand remark before she switched her attention elsewhere, she was holding his gaze. 'I mean I don't know much about the business,' he went on, 'but I'd imagine it can put a bit of a strain on you.' That had been enough patter, he judged, to really let the old PL shine in there and persuade

101

Debbie about his personal charisma. She was looking at him with a tiny frown, the way he imagined some women would look at objects of worship.

'Lofty,' she said hesitantly.

He imagined the light flooding out of him. 'Yes, Debbie?'

'Don't think I'm being too personal . . .'

'Be as personal as you like,' he said, for once not minding what he said to her in front of Andy.

Debbie moistened her lips. 'I think you should get your glasses checked.'

'Pardon?'

'Your eyes – they've gone all sort of squinty.'

Lofty moved back smartly from the bar. 'Excuse me. Customer waiting.' He hurried through to the other bar, feeling his cheeks burn. Dumb move, he kept thinking as he served Pete Beale and the man with him. Dumb, dumb move. He'd gone into action too soon. He should have waited another week or two until he'd got the technique down pat. He glanced past the partition and saw Andy grinning as Debbie whispered to him, her shoulders quaking. God, he thought, *what a dumb move!*

'How much'll that be then, Lofty?'

He realized Pete was waiting to pay. 'Oh. Sorry. It's, ah, one sixty-two, please.'

Pete counted out the right money then led his companion to a table in the corner. As they sat down the other man was careful to angle his chair so that he would face Pete squarely.

'Cheers,' Pete mumbled, taking a sip from his glass.

The other man said nothing. He took three

102

mouthfuls, keeping his eyes on Pete. When he put down his glass he wiped his mouth with the back of his hand. 'I'm not viewing this as a social encounter, Mr Beale. The pub's no more than a convenient place for us to talk.'

'I know that.'

'So let's talk.' He pulled a wad of folded papers from his inside pocket and slapped them on to the table. 'You know what these are, don't you?'

'I've a rough idea.'

'And you know who I am, I take it?'

Pete nodded. They had never met before, but there had been correspondence. This was Max McGinley, a debt collector with a reputation to strike terror into the heart of any failing trader. Pete took in the man's tidy haircut, the completely civilized set of his features, the crisp white collar and dark tie. Only the eyes gave him away. He looked at Pete with the kind of determination that would find no means too extreme. McGinley was a headhunter.

'These bills are owed to four separate wholesalers, Mr Beale. They add up to more than a thousand pounds.'

'I'm well aware of that.'

McGinley's forearm slid across the table like a foraging snake. The fingertips stopped on the edges of the bills. 'You're also aware that I've been retained to collect the money. I've written to you three times. You haven't replied.'

'I've been tryin' to get the cash together . . .'

'No,' McGinley said flatly. 'You haven't. You've been carrying on business as usual. You've been running up bills with other unsuspecting suppliers, getting yourself in deeper and playing the usual loser's game of hoping something'll turn up in the meantime.' He dislodged something from a tooth before he went on. 'You'll forgive me for speaking so bluntly. It's time for bluntness. That's why I came to find you in person.'

Pete's uneasiness was too generalized to let him feel anything in particular. He had been on his way home when the long black car had drawn up beside him, like a Mafia limousine. He had suggested they talk in the pub because he didn't want McGinley going to the house. For as long as he could, he would keep his home a sanctuary. It was practically all that was left.

'What exactly are you plannin' to do, Mr McGinley?'

The man looked offended. 'That's *my* question,' he pointed out. 'I want to know your proposals for clearing this debt.'

'I . . .' Pete shifted in his seat. 'I'll need a bit of time to work somethin' out . . .'

'Time? How about the time between now and when I get up to walk out that door? You've already had more time than you ever deserved.'

'Look . . .' Pete glanced to either side and leaned closer. 'I'm knockin' meself out puttin' a new business together. The bloody consortium's near enough ruined me an' I'm doin' what I can to fight back. I've got to buy stock an' I've got a family to look after, so I need every penny I get . . .'

'My clients need their money too, Mr Beale. Their

interests are my primary consideration. Your hard-luck story might help you to borrow funds, but it certainly won't help you to side-step your debts.'

Pete stared across the pub, feeling the strangeness, the sense of isolation from everything and everyone around him. The truth was focusing more tightly now. He was in the clutches of a collector. The worst collector of the lot. And he hadn't anything to throw him, not one scrap that would divert him for even a second.

'So?' McGinley urged. 'Have you any assets that can be turned into cash?'

'Nothin' I can think of.'

'What about the van?'

'It's not mine. It's on loan.'

'Household effects?'

Pete stared at him. 'I can't go plunderin' my wife's possessions, can I?'

'There are ways of forcing the issue,' McGinley said. His finger tapped the bills. 'These have to be paid. We're not open to negotiation on the point.' He picked up his glass, gazed at the contents for a second, then emptied it. 'I think you've got the picture, Mr Beale, and if I've managed to give you some sense of urgency, at least my journey won't have been wasted.' He stood up. 'Don't feel relieved I'm going. Because I'll come back, soon. When I do, I'll require a proposal for repayment – plus some proof that you'll carry it out.'

Pete stood up too. 'Can you tell me what kind of time I'll have to pay?'

'We'd prefer the cash in a lump. If that isn't

possible, then the minimum repayment period acceptable to my clients would be six weeks.'

Pete's mind raced. Six weeks, with nearly eleven hundred pounds owing. he stared at McGinley. 'That's – that's a hundred-an'-eighty-odd a week.'

'I believe so.'

'But I can't raise that kind of cash . . .'

McGinley sniffed delicately. 'I told you before, about your hard-luck story. I'm not interested.' He turned to the door. 'I'll give you until Tuesday, Mr Beale.'

'One thing . . .'

'Yes?'

'What happens if I can't come up with the goods?'

McGinley looked at the polished toes of his shoes for a moment. 'Lots and lots of unpleasant things can happen,' he said, without a trace of menace in his voice. 'Best you think along other lines, because I promise you this – I *will* get my clients' money back.'

It was nearly another hour before Pete felt he could leave the pub. The experience with the debt collector had left him drained and frightened. If he had been confronted by a big thug who'd threatened him with physical violence, he wouldn't have felt half so bad. He would have fought. But what he had just gone through was different. McGinley's dark confidence had cut his spirit. Men like that always won.

As Pete finally left to go home, Ali and Sue Osman were taking their drinks to a table. Sue eased herself into a corner of the padded upholstery and groaned.

'I feel like I've been draggin' this about for years.' She shifted her knees until the hump under her smock was more comfortable. 'I'll be glad when I've unloaded it.'

Ali had heard it all before, practically every day for the past month. Nevertheless he pretended to be amused. 'The nice thing is,' he murmured, sliding his stool close to the table, 'that way, you lose all your extra weight at once.'

'It might be a joke to you, but it ain't for me.' She tasted her fruit juice and made a face. 'Yuch. Nothin' tastes right any more, neither.'

'That'll pass, love.' Ali hoped it would all pass, her moaning, her complaining, her constant need to create strife between them. Just lately, she had made life close to impossible for him. 'You'll see things differently when you've had the baby.'

'I see things differently already.' She looked about her suddenly, sniffing the air. She made another face. 'Somebody's smokin' a pipe.'

'What do you mean, you see things differently already?'

'Oh, I've had time to take stock when I've been restin' in the afternoons. It's funny how, when you're busy all the time, a lot of things get past you and you don't notice.'

Ali had a feeling she was talking about him again. He decided to change the topic. 'We did pretty good business today, Sue. Well up on this time last year. I reckon it'll be no time at all before the cafe's takin' a handsome profit.'

'You'll know the day when it happens,' she

grunted. 'There'll be a pig flyin' over the railway bridge.'

Ali bit his tongue. There was no sense in arguing with her, just as there seemed to be no point humouring her, either. That afternoon he had watched her walking back to the house from the cafe. He had found himself seeing her objectively, a woman abandoning her youth too early, swopping it for the ageless, scowling bitchery that infested some other women around the square. She had lost her pride in her appearance and drew her only satisfaction from tearing holes in him and anybody else who measured up to her scorn. The preciousness had gone out of her, and he didn't think it was just the pregnancy that had made the change. Sue was already an apprentice battleaxe.

'Mind if I join you?'

Ali looked up and saw Debbie Wilkins. Any distraction was welcome, even the girl his wife thought was a stuck-up, toffee-nosed little cow. 'Not at all,' Ali said brightly. 'Sit down.'

Debbie took a stool, smoothing her skirt carefully as she sat down. Ali couldn't help making the comparison; on one side of the table was this highly feminine, shapely, pretty-faced young woman, on the other was his personal dragon, shapeless and dishevelled, frowning at the newcomer.

'Andy's gone off on night shift,' Debbie explained. 'I didn't feel like going home just yet, but I hate sitting alone in a bar.' She flashed a smile at Sue. 'You do when you're a woman, don't you?'

'I suppose so,' Sue said flatly.

Debbie sipped daintily from her glass and looked

at Ali again. 'How's business going? Prospering, are you?'

'I was just sayin' to Sue, we're startin' to do really well.' He grinned at his wife, feeling his cordiality being shot down a foot from her face. 'It's early days yet, but I reckon we'll make a go of it. Won't we, love?'

'Will we?' Sue snatched up her glass, drank and made a face.

'I always think it's very brave of people, starting their own businesses,' Debbie chirped. 'Especially in the present economic climate.'

'Daft's more like the word for it,' Sue snapped. 'You're best stayin' where you are, all cosy an' coddled in your bank.'

'Oh, it's far from being like that.' Debbie's smile was becoming fixed. 'We've a lot of responsibility, and there are plenty of penalties for people who don't pull their weight.'

'Fascinatin'.' She swallowed the rest of her drink and struggled to her feet.

'What are you doin'?' Ali asked her.

'I'm goin' home.' She pulled and grunted her way around the table. 'I'm tired.'

'But we just got here,' Ali complained. 'You said you fancied an evenin' in the pub.'

'Well I've changed me mind.' She waddled a few steps towards the door and paused. 'You stop if you want to. I'm sure there's plenty to keep you occupied.' She turned away without glancing at Debbie. They watched her push her way through the door and disappear on to Bridge Street.

'I'm sorry,' Ali said. 'It's her condition . . .'

'That's all right,' Debbie said primly. 'I understand.'

'I'd better go after her.' Ali finished his drink and got up. 'Sorry to leave you stranded like this.' He shrugged awkwardly. 'It can't be helped.'

'Don't worry about it. I'll have Angie to talk to when she's not so busy.'

'Right. See you.' Ali hurried out. On Bridge Street he looked about wildly. There was no sign of Sue. He couldn't understand where she'd gone in just a few seconds. Then he saw the elbow of her smock, jutting out at the corner of the pub.

When he got to her she was leaning on the tiled wall, her hand pressed to her mouth. She was crying.

'Oh, love . . .' Ali closed his arms around her. 'What is it?'

She put her head on his shoulder, unable to speak for the sobbing.

'Ssh, Sue darlin', don't take on like that.' He stroked her dry, wispy hair. 'Come on, what is it?'

She looked up at him, her face contorted and tear-tracked. 'I'm frightened, Ali.'

'What've you got to be frightened about? Is it the baby? Are you frightened to have it?'

She shook her head. 'Me. I'm frightened about me.' A long, low wail escaped as she let him draw her closer. 'What's happenin' to me? I can't help it, it's happenin' an' I can't stop it.'

Ali folded her tightly in his arms, nuzzling her face softly with his chin. 'It'll be all right, love. It'll all change soon.' He stared at the wall behind her and prayed it was true. As the moments passed and her tears warmed the front of his shirt, he felt the

110

slow dawning of consolation. This one little breach in her hardness had begun to melt him. She was his again, she was his precious Sue. For a while there, he thought he'd lost her for good.

On Monday, after a weekend and a morning agonizing over his plight, Pete Beale tightened his courage and went to see the bank manager.

He had to wait twenty minutes in the banking hall, watching cash deposits and withdrawals that would have solved his problems a dozen times over. At last a clerk ushered him into the manager's empty office and told him to take a seat. Two more nerve-shredding minutes passed before the manager made his entrance, carrying a folder with Pete's name on the front. The man was small, plump and pink-faced, with a mouth puckered by years of condescending disapproval. As he sat down he issued a fleeting, taut smile, which was as much as his double-breasted smugness would permit him.

After an awkward opening exchange, the manager sat back and let Pete outline his predicament. He explained about the drop in business, his change of trading method and the encumbrance of his eleven-hundred pound debt. He finished by saying that he was in no position, currently, to pay the debt, even though he was being pressed for urgent settlement.

The manager nodded slowly and flipped open the file. For thirty seconds he read it in silence, then looked up.

'I must say I'm grateful that you've been so candid,' he murmured. 'Not many customers with your record would come here and make such a clean breast of things.'

'Well . . .' Pete shifted his feet awkwardly. 'I thought it was best you knew the whole picture.'

The manager nodded again and closed the file. 'Of course, we won't put undue pressure on you to clear the overdraft, in the circumstances. But I'm sure you'll agree some scheme for repayment should be worked out as soon as possible.'

Pete frowned at him. 'I'm sorry?'

'We have to stop the rot, don't we?' The little mouth resumed its pucker, waiting for Pete's response.

'I'm sorry, I don't think you understand what I – '

The manager interrupted by clearing his throat. 'You owe the bank money, Mr Beale. It's only a few hundred pounds and in ordinary circumstances, because you have an overdraft facility, we wouldn't press for payment. But after what you've disclosed to me, I must tell you that a recovery plan will have to be drawn up – something as painless as possible, of course.'

'But I came here to ask for your help.'

'Help?' It sounded as if he had never heard the word before.

'To pay my debts. I want to borrow the eleven hundred quid.'

The manager looked appalled. 'From *us*? But Mr Beale, you would be even further in our debt then, wouldn't you? And on your own admission, you can't even cope with ordinary household expenses. You've had to make cutbacks. With a picture like that, you surely couldn't expect the bank to lend you money?'

'Well . . .'

'You have nothing to secure such a loan. The repayments would be far beyond you, and with interest rates as high as they are . . .'

Pete sighed and stood up. 'I'm sorry I wasted your time.' He turned and walked to the door.

'Mr Beale . . .' The manager was halfway out of his chair. 'While you're here we should draw up an agreement on the repayment of your indebtedness to the bank.'

'I don't have the time,' Pete told him. He yanked open the door.

'Mr Beale! I have to protect the bank's position!'

'What about *my* position?' Pete demanded. 'I'm stretched out ready for crucifyin', an' you want me to help you bang in some of the nails.' He strode out and banged the door shut after him, leaving the manager to bump his fist petulantly on the desk.

Outside, with his mind set stiffly against the warnings he'd heard and the natural caution he felt, Pete headed for Dalmyre Road, a street of dour-fronted shops and offices twenty yards from the bank. At the corner he hesitated, fighting back new, urgent thoughts of what he might be throwing himself into. 'Sod it!' He slammed his mind shut and briskly began walking again.

The loan office was smaller than its frontage suggested. It was very bare, too. There was only a counter with a brass bell, and beyond that a desk, a swivel chair and a filing cabinet. Pete took a deep breath and tapped the bell. The sound seemed to fill the room, like a jarring warning to get out of there.

A woman appeared from a tiny room beyond. She was middle-aged and dressed in a thick sweater, tweed skirt and brogue shoes. To Pete she looked more like a dog breeder than a money-lender. He had expected something male, oily and dangerous-looking.

'Can I help you?' She sounded quite pleasant. There was even the trace of a smile.

Pete told her he had come to enquire about a loan.

'What figure do you have in mind?'

'Fifteen hundred.' If he was going to get wet at all, he thought, it might as well be at the deep end.

The woman nodded as casually as if he had said fifteen pounds. 'If I could have a few details,' she said, taking a form and a pen from the desk. 'Can we start with your name?'

They continued with his address, occupation, approximate income and estimated weekly outgoings. He took care to double the figure of his earnings and cut a quarter off the household bills. He also implied, heavily, that his two business outlets meant his trade was actually expanding. The procedure seemed to be going very well. The woman wrote down the particulars in a dispassionate, unhesitating manner until all the questions had been answered. Then she read the form over to herself and smiled at Pete.

'There,' she said. 'That was pretty painless, eh?'

'Absolutely,' he said, smiling back. After all he'd heard, it had turned out to be a piece of cake. He

114

wondered if they kept the cash on the premises, or if he had to wait a day or two.

The woman turned to the desk and picked up another form. 'Would you sign this, please?'

Pete stared at the paper as she put it in front of him. He wasn't going to sign any receipt until he got the money. It didn't look like a receipt, though. 'What is it, love?'

'It's a form authorizing us to look into your affairs.'

'Me affairs?'

She nodded.

'What . . . Uh, what does that mean, exactly?'

'Well, we need to confirm the details you've just given me, to satisfy ourselves that you're in a sound way of business. We'd also get what we call your social profile – our enquiries are very discreet, of course.'

'Oh. I see.'

'You can understand we have to do this, Mr Beale. It's all designed to safeguard our own business. While I'm sure you're a perfectly honest man, you can appreciate that we can't take a potential client's word for anything.'

'Sure. It's an obvious precaution.' It seemed crazy, suddenly, that he should have had misgivings about coming near a place like this. He was in less danger of getting into a nasty fix with a money-lender than most people – because he had less chance than most people of getting a loan.

'I've had a thought,' he said, after staring at the form for a few more seconds. 'I should really consult my wife before I take a step like this. I mean it wouldn't be fair, would it, not lettin' her know . . .'

He saw a change come over the woman. She'd heard that one before, he supposed. And she would always have heard it at the point whem she sprung the consent form on the applicant.

'If you don't mind,' he went on, 'I'll nip home an' discuss it with her.'

'Whatever you say, Mr Beale.' She held up the application form. 'If you don't come back, I'll destroy this.' Her eyes hardened a little more. 'Unless you want to do it yourself, of course.'

'Ah, well . . .' She had him taped, all right. Nobody wanted his lie sheet left behind in a place he had no intention of going back to. 'Can I take it with me, just to show the wife how straightforward the drill is?'

'Of course.'

Seconds later he was back on the street, still seeing the woman's face, her eyes flatly accusing above the smile. The image vanished as he realized he was out of options. He was back where he had been all weekend.

But there was one meagre bonus. Those two stressful encounters had done something for him. It would be a shade easier, now, to face Max McGinley. And he was going to do that now. He wasn't prepared to go through another day of aching black dread.

He crossed the road to the Post Office, checked the address in the telephone directory, then set off, trying again – with less success this time – to keep his mind closed to all the glinting fears about his future.

McGinley was surprised to see him. He offered Pete a chair and even a cup of coffee. Pete could have used the coffee, but he knew his hand would shake too much to let him drink it.

'I've just had one, thanks,' he said.

The debt collector turned from the percolator and eased one haunch on to the edge of the desk. 'What have you come to tell me?'

The man had a terrible stillness, Pete thought. It opposed the power of speech. Pete cleared his throat. 'I've been to the bank,' he said. 'An' I've been to see a money-lender. No dice, either place. Short of doin' a robbery, I can't raise the cash.'

McGinley altered the position of his shoulders. Otherwise there was no visible change in him. His face remained calm. 'So how about being able to make the instalments we discussed?'

'I've spent days tryin' to think of a way. But there's none. I couldn't come up with that kind of money. Not even if I gave you every penny I earned.'

The desk creaked softly as McGinley stood up. 'Then you leave me no alternative, Mr Beale. The machinery to recover your debt will have to be set in motion.'

Pete had heard that when people were told, after months of worry, that they had a fatal disease, their first reaction was relief. He understood that now. He passed a hand across his forehead and felt cold sweat.

'What happens, Mr McGinley?'

'My clients get their money. You do some suffering.' McGinley went behind the desk. 'I don't think we've any more to say to each other.' He sat down and drew the telephone towards him. 'If you'll excuse me, I've a couple of calls to make.'

Pete stood up. His legs felt very weak. Even in that condition, though, he knew he could pick up the debt collector and throw him around the office. He was strong enough to hammer him to a pulp. He also knew, with the deepest certainty, that it would get him nowhere, except deeper in trouble. And he was miles deeper now than he should ever have let himself sink. Wondering how he would tell Kathy what they were facing now, he turned and left the office, hearing the purr of the telephone dial as he went.

Arthur Fowler had stayed chatting too long with a couple of old mates down at the Job Centre. Now he was late for tea. All the way down Bridge Street he could see the spectre of Pauline, giving him a tongue-whacking for letting his meal get ruined. She'd been edgy enough lately, without this aggravation. Arthur was rehearsing an apology when he spotted Pauline, in her apron and slippers, standing on the corner by number 45. She was staring in the direction of Dr Legg's surgery.

She turned as Arthur approached.

'Sorry I'm late, love. I was followin' up another job lead. What're you doin' out here, anyway?'

'I was lookin' for Mark,' she said. 'But I've found him.' She pointed. The boy was leaning on the post at the top of the surgery stairs. 'I shouted to him a couple of times, but he hasn't heard me.'

'Hoi!' Arthur yelled, making Pauline jump. 'Mark!'

The boy didn't move. He remained where he was, hands in pockets, ankles crossed.

'Mark!' Arthur shouted again. There was still no response. He turned to Pauline. 'What's up with him? Gone bloody deaf or somethin'?'

'How should I know?'

'You go in,' Arthur said. 'I'll fetch him.'

He was fifteen feet away when he realized something really was wrong. From the corner Mark's expression had looked normal. Now Arthur could see his head was back against the pillar and he was staring at the sky. He was grinning fixedly. Nearer still, Arthur saw the saliva dripping from his chin.

Arthur dashed forward and grabbed him by the shoulders. 'What's wrong with you, for God's sake?' He shook the boy and his head lolled forward. He moaned softly and tried to pull away. 'Mark! Speak to me, will you?'

Mark giggled and swung one arm free. He waved it limply above his head. 'Fabulous, huh?' His head came round and he stared at his father. 'Better'n walkin',' he sniggered.

'What?'

Mark's head rolled sideways and back, striking the concrete post.

'Christ almighty . . .' Arthur grabbed the boy's arm and pulled it across his shoulders. Mark began giggling again as his father dragged him towards the house.

Pauline turned from the cooker as they came barging in through the back door.

'What's happened to him?' She watched Arthur ease their son down on to a chair. Mark wasn't grinning any more. His face had turned very serious. He looked from his mother to his father, then slowly closed his eyes.

'I know what's bloody happened to him an' so do you,' Arthur hissed. 'Shut that kitchen door. We don't want Mum or Michelle seein' him in this state.'

For five minutes they shook the boy to keep him awake and steadily mopped his face with cloths soaked in cold water. Quite suddenly Mark sat upright in the chair, his eyes moving wildly.

'He's havin' a fit!' Pauline squeaked. 'God, what'll we do, Arthur?'

As they stared at him, Mark gasped, shut his eyes tightly and vomited.

The door to the living room burst open and Lou came in. She stared at Mark, horrified. 'What's up with the poor lamb?'

'He's only been sick, Mum,' Pauline said, grabbing the wet cloths from the drainer as Arthur hoisted the boy and draped him by the sink. 'Go an' sit down, we'll see to him.'

'But shouldn't you get the doctor?'

'We'll get him if he's needed,' Arthur snapped. 'Make some room an' let us get the lad cleaned up, eh?'

Reluctantly Lou went. Pauline dug around in the washing basket and fished out a clean pair of pyjamas. 'These ain't been ironed yet, but they'll do.'

When Mark had been sponged down and his soiled school uniform taken off, they managed to get him into the pyjamas and back on to the chair. He had calmed now and appeared to be coming round.

'Right,' Arthur muttered to Pauline. 'No more pretendin', eh? I know about this drugs business. Dr Legg told me.'

Pauline looked at him sheepishly for a moment, then she sighed. 'I wasn't tryin' to do anythin' behind your back, Arthur, I was tryin' to keep you from any more worryin' . . .'

'I know that. No need to explain.' He peered at Mark. 'I reckon he'll be all right now.' He straightened and buttoned his jacket. 'I'm off out. I'll be back soon as I can.'

'Where are you goin'?'

'To put the kybosh on this, once an' for all.'

'Arthur – '

'Just get him to bed, Pauline. I'll talk to you after.'

For fifteen minutes Arthur toured the local pubs, asking after Nick Cotton, feeling his anger sharpen every time he drew a blank. As he strode from place to place he kept picturing the same thing: the shifty-eyed Nick passing poison to his son with one hand and taking money with the other. The obscenity of the tableau grated on an un-named nerve, somewhere close to Arthur's sense of outrage. On his way back to the house, having located his target in none of the places he'd looked, he paid another call at The Vic, just in case. The first person he saw was Nick Cotton. He was standing by the bar talking to Angie and being carefully monitored, a few feet away, by Den.

Arthur stomped forward and slapped a hand on Nick's leather shoulder. 'Pardon me cuttin' in, Ange. I want a word with this one.'

'What's the bloody game?' Nick demanded. He tried to brush Arthur's hand away, but found it was clamped too firmly. 'This is a technical assault, know that?'

'So charge me.' With his free hand Arthur jerked a thumb at the door. 'Outside,' he growled. 'Now.'

'Don't you order me about!'

'*Now!*'

Nick glared at Angie. 'Do you allow this kind of thing in here?'

Den came forward like a shot. 'We allow your kind of thing in here, sunshine, so I suppose anythin' goes.' He winked at Arthur. 'Don't do anythin' I wouldn't, eh? That should give you a fair bit of scope.'

Arthur yanked hard on Nick's sleeve. 'I only want a couple of minutes of your time.' He moved towards the door and Nick went with him. 'Sorry for the disturbance, Den and Angie. It won't happen again.'

Outside Nick shook his arm free. 'This is a dead liberty,' he blustered. 'I can get a bit of private action taken, if you don't watch it.'

Arthur put a hand on Nick's chest and pushed him against the wall. 'Shut it and listen.'

Nick jutted his chin. 'All right, I'll listen. But you've been warned . . .'

'An' you're about to get warned.' Arthur looked about him. There was no one else on Bridge Street.

'This is a threat, actually, not a warnin'. If you ever put drugs anywhere near the reach of my son again, I'll batter you shitless. I'll maim you. Is that clear?'

Nick tried to look indignant and menacing at the same time. The result was a kind of facial uneasiness. 'I don't have no dealin's with drugs. Never have done.'

'There's nothin' nasty you don't have dealin's with. We both know that.'

'You're talkin' bollocks!'

'I'll be kickin' bollocks if you don't take note of what I've said.' Arthur poked Nick sharply on the breastbone. 'Keep drugs away from our Mark – keep your stinkin' *self* away from him.' He pushed his face very close. 'You'd be astonished at what I'd do to protect me own. An' don't go dreamin' up any hard-man threats. You're a turd, nothin' more or less. I don't mind steppin' on the odd piece of shit if it'll keep somebody else from gettin' fouled.' He stood back. 'End of interview. Piss off.'

He waited until Nick did his best to swagger away, then he crossed the road and let himself into the yard at number 45. By the back door he paused, thinking. For nearly half an hour he had let a powerful paternal impulse dominate him. He had let it turn his thinking from the way of reason, which he favoured, to the way of violence, which he would have followed all the way if he'd been sure Nick Cotton was guilty. Even though he had known in advance he might follow that route, Arthur was surprised how easily he took to it.

He turned away from the door and crossed the

road, heading for the pub again. He needed breathing space to think things out. A pint might help. It might give him the time to get back inside his peaceful view of life, before he tackled Mark about the stupidity of giving in to dangerous impulses.

Pete was surprised to find the padlock undone. He pulled open the door, stepped into the lock-up and gazed about him, feeling for a moment that he was in the wrong place. This was supposed to be where he kept the van. What confronted him was nothing familiar. It was a mess, a chaos of disruption.

'Oh, no . . .' He stepped back into the open doorway, seeing the late sunlight dapple the wrecked van, the broken and splintered boxes, the scattered fruit and vegetables. 'Christ, *no!*'

The van's tyres were slashed. The rear doors were hanging halfway off their hinges. The display framework had been pulled out and scattered like firewood across the floor. Crates and boxes were smashed and splintered. The stock was ruined. Fruit had been stamped on and pulped, vegetables had been shredded and squashed. The warm air was rich with the mingling odours of the destruction.

Pete groaned. It seemed an age since he had trudged up to the door, baleful and sickened by the long talk with Kathy, the explanations that had turned, by stages, into a hysterical row. Life had to go on, he'd told himself as he left the flat. The van would have to be got ready for tomorrow. Until he had opened the door he thought he had suffered more than his share of misfortune that day.

He turned and strode off to where the small van

was parked by the opposite wall. He got in and started it up, not caring now, not fearing for himself. He would show them what he was made of, he would do some smashing of his own and inflict hurt where it was most deserved. His foot rammed the accelerator and the van shot forward in a grinding shower of dirt and rubble.

Pete got to McGinley's place in less than ten minutes. It hadn't occurred to him, in his anger, that the debt collector might have gone home by now. When he twisted the handle the door wouldn't give. He rattled it furiously and kicked the frame. The sign said CLOSED. Pete kicked again and banged the glass panel with his fist. His frustration gathered in a sour knot at his throat as he almost wrenched the handle off.

He stopped suddenly, hearing movement inside. There was a shadow on the panel, moving. Bolts were being undone. The door swung open and McGinley stood there in his shirtsleeves.

'What the hell do you think you're doing?'

'You rotten bastard!'

Pete lunged at him and McGinley stepped back. Pete overbalanced, carried by his own bulk. He grabbed the door frame and swung again. Two surprisingly strong hands closed round his fist and he was pulled forward to his knees. Before he could adjust himself his hand was being twisted fiercely, the nerves in the wrist screaming with pain.

'Will you stop, or will I break it?'

Pete gasped, feeling the fire tear along his arm. He sagged, submitting, glaring his agonized hatred up at McGinley.

'That's better, Mr Beale.'

The pain dropped to a dull throb as Pete's hand was released. He pushed himself to his feet, knowing now he couldn't fight this man. 'You're still a bastard,' he hissed.

The debt collector stepped close for a moment then moved back. 'There's no smell of drink off you, so what's brought this on?'

'You know bloody well what!'

McGinley shook his head. 'I don't know,' he said quietly. 'Come into the office and tell me.' He turned his back on Pete and walked in ahead of him. Even the back, it seemed, was alert to any sudden movement. Pete leaned on the wall beside the desk, rubbing his wrist. McGinley stopped by the window and sat on the ledge. 'You didn't cut up rough earlier, when you might have. So why now?'

'The van. My stock – don't stand there an' tell me you don't know.'

McGinley's expression changed. His eyes, for once, were not on the attack. They were narrow, inquiring. 'I know nothing special about your van or your stock. Tell me what's happened.'

Pete was suddenly deflating. It was true, he could tell by looking at him; McGinley didn't know. 'The van's wrecked, my stock's been destroyed. I've been put out of business.'

McGinley sombrely processed the information. 'I see.' He pointed to a chair. 'Sit down while I pour us both a coffee.'

When they were facing each other across the desk, McGinley said, 'Tell me why you thought I was responsible.'

'Well, I've heard stories . . .'

'I've heard them too. My reputation more or less relies on them. A lot of the stories are true, as far as they go – some local people in debt *do* have violent things done to them and to their property. But I've never done any of those things. I've never hired people to do them, either. I operate my business well within the bounds of the law.'

Pete frowned at him. 'But you told me yourself – terrible things would happen to me, that's what you said.'

'The threat's the thing that often gets results, Mr Beale. But the terrible things *I* set in motion are done by the courts and the bailiffs.'

The wind was entirely gone from Pete's sails. He stared bleakly at the debt collector. 'So who the hell did this to me? And why?'

McGinley unclasped his hands, sat back and clasped them again. 'Why don't you have another coffee and tell me how your troubles began?' he said. 'I'm interested.'

July

Lofty believed that Persuasive Light was now entirely at his disposal. After one or two false starts, or perhaps nine or ten if he really counted them up, he felt the technique was second nature to him. Now, up and about on a bright Monday morning, he was going to put it to positive, dynamic use.

He strode into the Job Centre and went straight to the desk. The young woman there looked at him as if he had come to hold the place up.

'Can I help you?'

Lofty had his patter ready. He reasoned it made sense to use a line of chat that matched the strength of personality he was radiating. 'I believe *I* can help *you*,' he said, showing her the smile he had been rehearsing.

Now it looked like she though he might be a rapist. 'I don't understand,' she said stiffly.

'I want a job.'

'How would that help us?'

Lofty kept his gaze steadily on her, zapping out the PL. 'Whatever job you find me, I'll be a credit to you. This place'll go up in the employers' estimation. You know how word gets round.'

She had finally got him figured out. He was a nut case. 'It's good of you to favour us this way,' she murmured acidly. 'Have you had a look at the jobs on the cards over there?'

He shook his head. 'I want you to assess me. Fit me to the right job, you know?'

'We don't usually operate that way. We're not personnel officers.'

'Could you make an exception in this case?' His eyes were getting tired, but he went on gazing at her, letting her see his potential. 'I've really got a lot to offer to the right firm.'

The girl moved away from the counter. 'Hang on,' she said. 'I'll get someone to speak to you.' She went through to the office at the back and spoke to a man at a desk. 'There's a head-banger out there wants us to assess him for a job,' she muttered. 'Real weirdo. Stares all the time. Will you have a word with him?'

The man was fat and flustered, the kind of born clerk who could make every task look and sound like an extreme effort of stamina and will. 'Can't you handle it yourself, Miss Loxley? I'm very busy.'

'He doesn't look like he'll go away without making a scene. You know the way it can get when a screwy one turns up.'

The man sighed. 'I'm always the one who has to sort out the difficult cases.' He lumbered to his feet. 'I often wonder what you'd all do without me.' He shuffled out to the counter and scowled at Lofty. 'I'm Mr Hepton,' he snapped. 'What seems to be the trouble?'

'No trouble,' Lofty said, feeling his heart lift. He had only been there a minute or so and already they'd sent an expert to see him. This was PL in action, all right. 'I explained to the young lady, I'd like to be given a job that fits my kind of drive.'

Mr Hepton drummed his nail-bitten fingers on the counter. 'Getting a job these days,' he said officiously, 'isn't simply a matter of walking in here and being handed one. We have long waiting lists . . .'

'But I'd be an asset to somebody. There's an employer somewhere just waitin' for me.'

'Is that a fact?'

Lofty didn't catch the sarcasm. He was too busy sustaining the technique and the hyped-up way of talking.

'You should really go to the Social Security office, you know,' Hepton went on. 'I think they have the facilities there to set you on the right path.'

'Just try me with a job interview,' Lofty insisted. He hadn't expected it to be quite this hard. He wasn't used to insisting on anything.

Hepton's fingers drummed a little harder. He didn't like the way this character was staring at him. He looked like he could be dangerous. A flat insistence that he leave might trigger some bizarre, violent behaviour. An idea suddenly came to Hepton. 'Well,' he said, pretending to scan his memory files, 'as a matter of fact, there *is* a vacancy that might be just the thing for you. Wait there.'

He went through to the back and winked at Miss Loxley. 'I'll soon sort out this clown,' he wheezed. 'Where's the details of that processing plant job?'

'What – Lambert's?'

'That's the one.'

'Nobody ever stays there.' She wrinkled her nose. 'Can't say I blame them. He'll be back in ten minutes.'

'So what? It'll get him out of our hair for the time being. And it'll buy us a bit of extra time, anyway.' Hepton shuffled the papers around on the desk and fished out a card. 'Right.' He grinned at the card as if it were an accomplice. 'Let's fix our bright boy up with the job of a lifetime.'

When Lofty spotted the card his heart did another little flutter. There it was, proof, if proof were needed, that PL was all it was cracked up to be. They had found him something already.

'This should be just the thing,' Hepton said, smiling. He handed the card to Lofty. 'If you go to the address at the top and ask for the manager, I think they'll be able to take you on.'

'Can I go right away?'

'No, no, I was coming to that. They only interview every other Monday. So you'll have to wait until next week.' He leaned closer. 'Confidentially, I've let you in on this ahead of quite a few others.'

Lofty read the name. Lambert Specialities (Walford) Ltd. He looked at Hepton again. 'You reckon this place'll be right for me?'

'Oh yes. I've got an eye for a man's potential. That job will fit you to perfection. That's why I'm bending the rules.'

Lofty beamed. 'Great. What kind of job is it, exactly?'

'You'd be working in a branch of the chemical refinement and manufacturing industry. There's scope for pretty rapid promotion in that line, you know.'

Lofty thanked him warmly. 'I won't be a bad advertisement for you,' he promised. He shook

Hepton's hand before he thanked him again and left.

Hepton smiled slowly. When you worked in a Job Centre, he was thinking, you eventually came across every shape and shade of wally.

Water restrictions and hosepipe bans had been imposed early in the month, because the weather had been the driest since the drought of 1976. Not long after, a large area of Britain was shaken by the biggest earthquake to hit the country in a hundred years. Ethel Skinner chose to see all this as a vivid omen of change.

'Whether it's goin' to be a change for the better or for the worse, there's no sayin',' she told Lou Beale. 'But there's goin' to be big changes all round. Mark my words.'

They were standing by Pete's fruit and vegetable stall on Bridge Street. Until Ethel had arrived, Lou had been commiserating with Pete. He was running the stall again, leaving Kathy to do part-time work in a local bakery. As his mother tried to fend off Ethel and her talk of prognostications, Pete sidled away to re-arrange the meagre display on the stall.

'There's been droughts before,' Lou pointed out grumpily. 'I don't recall many big changes because of them – apart from there bein' more dust an' flies about than usual.'

'Ah,' Ethel said, raising a warning finger, 'but a drought *and* an earthquake, happenin' at the same time, now that's different. I know about these things, Lou.'

'Well, if there's goin' to be big changes, I hope

some of them happen for our Pete there. Any change in his fortunes is bound to be for the better.'

'I could do a readin' with the cards for him,' Ethel offered. 'Then you'd know how things'll go.'

Lou shook her head. 'No. I don't want none of that, Et. It's hard enough livin' with things the way they are. If they're goin' to get no better, I don't want to know.'

'But they might get better,' Ethel said. She loved doing card readings, but she would never do them without consent. 'Why not let me give it a whirl?'

'I said no, an' that's what I meant. Let's leave bad enough alone.'

'Suit yourself,' Ethel sighed. She tugged on Willie's leash, pulling him away from a nasty-looking puddle he'd been sniffing. 'If folk don't want to avail themselves of me special powers, it's their own lookout.' She trotted away.

Lou turned to Pete, who was pushing empty boxes under the barrow. 'There's times I wonder why I have anythin' to do with that silly old windbag,' she muttered.

Pete straightened up and smiled at her. 'She's your friend, Mum. She's been a mate of yours since forever.'

Lou scowled for a moment, then nodded. 'That's true enough. There's been times I'd have been lost without her.' She glanced at the display on the stall. 'It'll take more than Ethel's witchcraft to help us out of this mess, though.'

'It's my problem, Mum, not yours.'

'We're a family,' she said sternly. 'We share our good times an' our bad.'

Pete leaned on the stall and stuck his hands in his pockets. His mother saw resignation in the way he did that. She read thickening despair in most things he did nowadays. 'It's certainly a bit of a comfort to know there's others concerned for us,' he said.

Lou moved closer, lowering her voice even though there was no one nearby to hear them. 'What was you sayin' just then, before Ethel butted in?'

'About Rob Burkett? Oh, it's just that he's been so good about what happened to the van. The way he looks at it, he hardly ever used it anyway, an' he's quite happy to wait until I can get it fixed.'

'Don't the insurance cover it?'

'No. He wasn't covered for that kind of disaster – not while the van was in my possession, anyway.'

Lou was tempted to give him a lecture on insurance. For years she had told Pete and Kathy they should have more policies. Lou believed strongly that people had to keep themselves covered as much as possible, misfortune being as prevalent it was. But insurance had always been something Pete was considering. It was never anything he would get around to organizing. If he'd been properly covered, there would at least have been some compensation for the stock he lost.

'Mum . . .' Pete took his hands from his pockets and folded his arms. Lou saw that as a defensive move. 'There's a decision I've been puttin' off an' puttin' off – but it can't be avoided now. It's not somethin' you're goin' to like.'

'Then you better tell me quick an' get it over with.'

'It's the business. The stall. I'm goin' to have to close down.'

'What?' Lou stared at him. 'You'll do nothin' of the sort!'

'I can't do anythin' else.'

Lou couldn't have been more incensed if he had slapped her. 'This stall has stood on this site since before the war. Apart from the time when I had to shut down durin' the shortages, it's been here for fifty years an' more.'

'But Mum – '

'Beale's Fruit an' Veg is part of Walford history. An' it's stayin' a part of it.'

'Listen. Let me have my say. There's no money left to stock up. I'm strugglin' just to put on this lousy display. An' even if I'd twice the stock it'd make no difference, because people don't buy from me any more.'

'I've heard all that already – '

'An' it's all true. It's madness to try any more. I've only been keepin' the stall goin' these past weeks because I didn't want to break your heart. But facts have got to be faced, Mum. Honest to God, I'd keep goin' if I could, but it's impossible.'

Whenever Lou was faced with a reasonable, unassailable argument that went against her own stubborn views, she had one course of action and only one. She took it now. She turned and walked away.

Pete dug his hands into his pockets again. He had known she would react that way. He could have softened the blow, he supposed, by letting her know just how bad things really were for him; that way, her sympathy would have diluted her sense of affront. But it would have been unkind to do that. The extra worry, on top of her sorrow over the closure of the stall, would have crushed her.

Pete reached into his inside pocket and pulled out the latest piece of misery to shoot through the letterbox. All the staring in the world wouldn't make it go away, but he kept looking at it anyway, like someone prodding a painful tooth with his tongue. It was a summons. He would be in the debtors' court within the month. McGinley didn't waste any time. Pete had thought, ten days before when he had sat and talked to the debt collector, that the man had softened towards him. But it appeared not; perhaps he just liked hearing about people's woes. Justice was rolling steadily towards Pete like a bulldozer.

The bank hadn't wasted time, either. Tucked away in a drawer in the flat was a letter outlining the kind of action they proposed taking to get their money back. That would mean another summons, sooner or later. There would be one from the Council soon, too, because they had fallen behind with the rates on the flat.

Pete had tried to find ways of slowing the decay. He had tried to get a job at Covent Garden, he had tried for a dustman's job, he had even answered an advertisement for a washer-up in a hotel, but nobody wanted to know him. Bad luck had a way of affecting a man's style, he guessed. Nobody wanted to invite a Jonah on to their work force.

'Mornin', Pete,' Den had just opened up. He came across, eyeing the display, comparing its dismal proportions with Pete's expression. 'Any clues yet about who worked you over?'

Pete shook his head. 'The police are still on to it, but they've come up with nothin' so far.'

'Useless buggers.' Den picked up an apple and flipped a ten pence piece at Pete. 'I'll have this for me breakfast.'

'Breakfast? Bit late, isn't it?'

Den jerked a thumb over his shoulder. 'Her ladyship's got a hangover. I didn't fancy stayin' around the kitchen with her in that state.'

'Been hittin' it hard again, has she?'

'Drinkin' with both hands,' Den said.

'What's the problem this time?'

Den shrugged. 'Me, I suppose. It's always me, isn't it?'

'You an' your little pastime.'

Den took a bite from the apple and chewed it thoughtfully. 'For a while there, I thought we'd got it all sorted out. You know, Angie acceptin' things the way they are. Now I'm not so sure. She can be all right for a week or two, then she takes a nose-dive.'

Miserable as he was, Pete grinned. 'I really don't know how you cope. I mean, *two* women . . .'

'You're always sayin' that. An' I keep tellin' you the same thing. It's not a question of copin'. It ain't a chore, is it? I'm only doin' what most blokes would like to do. They'd all be at it if they had the bottle.' He winked. 'That's the secret. Bottle. An' no phoney sentimentality about the little woman at home.'

'It's not somethin' I'd want to do.' Pete said it

137

automatically, defensively. He wasn't sure if it was true, but he didn't ever want to question himself on the topic. 'My wife's enough for me.'

'Good. If you're content that way, it's the way to stay. But what if you weren't content? What would you do? Put up with life the way it is, instead of makin' it the way it should be?'

'I haven't thought about it.' Pete wasn't keen on pursuing this line, but at least it took his mind off his afflictions. 'Don't you ever worry about what it might do to Sharon, if she ever found out? Things like that can be tough on a kid.'

'Shar's fine.'

'But what if she finds out?'

'She won't.' Den bit another chunk out of the apple. 'She's too busy tryin' to get herself a boyfriend to bother with Angie an' me, anyway.'

'Maybe you're right.'

Pete had inadvertently brought back some of his own pain by mentioning Den's child. His own son, he knew, was suffering because of what was happening. Kathy was permanently short-tempered with him these days; Pete was too preoccupied to talk to the boy or spend time with him. He recalled how Ian had looked the night before, when he had walked into the flat while they were having another one of their don't-blame-me-because-we're-skint rows. They had stopped suddenly, seeing the boy in the doorway. He had tried to look as if he hadn't heard, but there was terrible anxiety in his eyes.

Pete shook the recollection aside. 'I've just broke it to Mum,' he said. 'About shuttin' down.'

'I'll bet *that* took a bit of bottle,' Den grunted.

'I'll say. She took it bad. Went off in a huff. But there's nothin' else for it, she'll have to accept what's inevitable.'

Den nodded sympathetically. 'So what's in prospect? Anythin'?'

Pete considered the onrush of financial ruin and family disruption. He stood to lose everything, the way he had once before, many years ago. 'Prospects, Den?' he said. 'Let me put it this way. From the gutter where I am, to where I'm goin', definitely ain't an upward journey.'

The bright shop front of T.F. Jennings and Sons was flanked by hanging baskets filled with flowers. In front of the well-stocked windows there were rows of boxes, lined with artificial turf and filled with apples, oranges, tangerines, bananas, melons and a bewildering variety of green vegetables.

Inside, the place was cool and pleasingly – if self-consciously – old-fashioned. There were two counters, immaculately varnished, running the entire length of the shop. The scales were the ancient Avery spring-operated type, white-enamelled with glistening chrome around the glass-fronted dials. The till was a reproduction of an early-thirties brass Hinkson, with gleaming filigree work along the back and side panels. The shelves were stacked with fruit and vegetables and there was a corner set aside for the sale of fresly cut flowers.

Max McGinley waited until one of the assistants was free, then he stepped forward and nodded politely. 'Would Mr Harris be available, I wonder?'

The girl nodded. 'I think he's free. Who shall I say wants to see him?'

McGinley gave his surname. 'If you'd tell him it's a personal matter, and rather urgent, I'd be obliged.'

The girl went away; she was back in less than a minute. 'Just go through the door at the end, sir. Mr Harris is in the office to the right.'

He followed her directions and found himself outside a door reminiscent of British hotel doors in old films. He tapped gently. A voice inside invited him to enter.

Harris was standing beside a filing cabinet, leafing through a sheaf of invoices. He was as tall as McGinley, with sandy hair and a face as old-fashionedly handsome as his shop. His moustache was tinged with white, giving him an air of para-military authority.

'Mr Harris? I'm Max McGinley.'

The tentatively welcoming smile slid away. 'Oh. *Max* McGinley. I've heard of you.' Harris put the papers on top of the cabinet. 'How can I help you? Denise said it was a personal matter. Urgent, apparently.'

McGinley nodded. 'I hope I'm not interrupting your work?'

'My meal breaks interrupt my work,' Harris said, smiling a little uneasily. 'I'm a workaholic, Mr McGinley. I thrive on hard graft and there's always plenty of it in this business for me to thrive on.' His accent was curious. It was suppressed Cockney with a not-very-intact gloss of BBC Newsreader.

'Well I'll be as brief as I can,' McGinley said. 'I'm

making enquiries concerning the business of a Mr Peter Beale.'

'Oh yes?' Keen interest replaced the caution in Harris's eyes. 'In some kind of trouble, is he?'

'With half the trouble he has,' McGinley said, 'he'd still be in pretty bad financial shape.'

'It doesn't surprise me.' Harris pointed to a chair by the desk. 'Take a seat.' He remained standing as McGinley sat down. 'The man, in my experience, hasn't the intelligence or flair to keep him off his knees for long. Have you been retained to, ah, shall we say extract settlement from him?'

'Yes, I have.'

'I don't envy him.' This time there was no uneasiness in the smile. It was wide and ingratiating. 'Your reputation for efficiency travels before you, Mr Mc – may I call you Max?'

'Of course.'

'Well, Max, I'd say your only problem with Beale will be the age-old one.'

McGinley's eyes narrowed a shade, expressing puzzlement.

'Getting blood out of a stone,' Harris explained. 'I don't know how much he owns in the way of cash or convertible assets, but I can't imagine it being much.'

'That's the impression I have, I must say.' McGinley shifted a fraction in his chair. It signalled a change in the drift of the conversation. 'The reason I'm here, Mr Harris, is directly connected with the fact that it was your consortium, or the consortium to which you belong, which put Mr Beale in his present predicamant.'

Harris spread his hands. 'Business is business, as I'm sure you, of all people, will appreciate.'

'Indeed I do. But it goes a little further than business in this case, I believe.'

Harris frowned. 'I don't follow.'

'You kept Beale out of the consortium, didn't you?'

'He would never have been allowed in – '

'Probably not, but you made it clear that you, personally, didn't want him to be even considered for membership.'

'Well . . .' Harris sniffed. 'Your homework is thorough enough, I'll say that. Yes, I did make it clear I wanted him kept out.'

'Because of an old vendetta.' McGinley spoke as if he were reading a charge sheet. 'A matter going back a number of years.'

'Yes, that's true. I don't forget, Max.' Harris tapped his head lightly. 'Every hurt I've been done is stored up here. I collect debts too, in my way.'

McGinley examined the nails of his right fingers for a moment. His eyes flicked up and met Harris's suddenly. 'You went a bit far this time though, didn't you? I mean, collecting interest the way you did . . .'

'I beg your pardon?'

'Mr Beale's van. His stock. You had someone do a wrecking job, didn't you?'

'That's ridiculous!'

McGinley shook his head slowly. His eyes were searching past Harris's, scanning the truth behind the mask of insult. 'I would have come to see you a lot sooner, except I had to get my suspicions confirmed. Today I managed to track down the people who actually destroyed that van and all of Mr Beale's stock. After a bit of initial reticence, they spoke to me freely. That kind usually do.'

'You're talking nonsense!' Harris's voice was slipping closer to its roots. 'What right do you think you have to come in here and talk to me like that? I can have you thrown out, you know.'

'But you won't.' McGinley stood up. 'As you said, you know my reputation. All aspects of it, I hope. What I'm proudest of is my thoroughness. I've got the goods on you, Mr Harris. Don't be foolish enough to doubt that.'

Harris was turning white. 'What have you come here for?'

'I thought that would be obvious,' McGinley said. 'I'm a debt collector, after all.'

At eleven o'clock on the morning when Lofty was due to present his talents to the management of Lambert Specialities (Walford) Limited, Nick Cotton was accosted by Mark Fowler in the saloon bar of *The Fox* on Carver Road. The timing was important. If anyone wanted to buy cannabis, uppers, downers or heroin, Nick's careful timetable had to be observed. He could be approached in *The Fox* between eleven and ten past on a Monday, or in *Jolly Jack's*, a Wapping pub, at two o'clock till closing time on Fridays. Numerous other privately organized deals were conducted throughout the week, but on Mondays and Fridays unscheduled purchases could be made. Nick was proud of his neatly organized sales system, but that morning he wasn't at all pleased to see Mark.

'I warned you before, kid. I can't do business with you.' Nick spoke almost without moving his lips, his eyes averted as if Mark weren't there.

'I just wanted one deal,' Mark said. 'One five quid deal, Nick.'

'I wouldn't handle it if it was a hundred quid deal,' Nick hissed. 'If you want any stuff, get it some place else.'

Mark looked round the room anxiously. It was a grubby place, populated by a sparse crowd of faceless, time-worn men in seedy clothes. Nobody with any self-respect ever went in there. It was not a pub geared for laughter or pleasure of any kind. *The Fox* was an enclosure for the sharing of moody discontent and social failure.

Mark hated the place. In truth there were things he hated about cannabis, too; he always managed, somehow, to overdose and make himself incapable or ill. But he hated being without the stuff. Cold reality was hard to take – harder, now, because he knew a useful escape route. Except Nick wasn't dealing with him any more.

'I've been gettin' it from a couple of other blokes,' he murmured. 'But they're screwin' me. One deal was cut with somethin' that made me sick as a pig. Another lot was fake.'

Nick sniffed. 'Beeswax.' He couldn't resist showing off his expertise, especially since he had so little. 'They melt it down an' mix in fibres off that hairy string you get.' He looked at Mark coldly. 'You've got to learn to spot these things, kid.'

'You deal in straight stuff, Nick. I'd rather just rely on you.'

'No dice. If you're worried about gettin' done, get your deals off a nigger. They'll always charge more, especially if you're white, but they'll never cheat you.' Nick looked at the clock. 'Do me a favour an' clear off, eh? You're hamperin' trade.' There were already a couple of men at the bar watching Nick cautiously. They were regulars. One of them had been buying from Nick for over a year.

'Please, Nick . . .'

'Listen.' Nick raised a warning finger, close to his own chest. 'I don't want you comin' anywhere near me, for any reason.'

'If it's my Dad you're worried about – '

'I'm not discussin' it. Clear off.'

Mark turned away dejectedly. As he passed the end of the bar the landlord reached across and tapped his shoulder. 'Keep out of here, son, will you?' It was worded as a request, but delivered like a firm instruction. 'I've enough to cope with without under-age drinkers hangin' about the place.'

'I wasn't drinkin',' Mark said.

'Less of the cheek or I'll clip your ear.'

Mark slouched off into the sunlight, sincerely wishing he was someone else. Anyone else would have done, anyone but this kid who got nothing but the thumbs-down from life. Rejection was all he ever came up against. His family brushed off any of his attempts to show he had a personality and opinions of his own; school teachers had long since eliminated the likelihood that there was anything of value between his ears; girls rebuffed him because he was shy and awkward; even the dregs, like that crummy landlord and shifty Nick Cotton, rejected him. At times Mark felt he was excluded from ordinary membership of the human race.

He headed in the general direction of Albert Square, not wanting to go there but lacking the urge to go anywhere else. There were still weeks of the summer holidays to kill. He had only a couple of mates and they were both off to Spain or somewhere with their families. The days seemed interminable and aimless. They were great stretches of flatness that had to be traversed whether he liked it or not. Passing the time with other people, like his parents, or his sister, or his cousin, or *anyone*, only led, one way or another, to some measure of rejection. He was stuck with his own company in a sea of idleness and boredom. If these were the happiest days of his life, he couldn't imagine how terrible it would be when he was grown up.

Except he didn't believe these were the best days. These were the worst. Youth, even for the luckiest of Mark's acquaintances, meant exclusion. There was a big, rich, fascinating world all around them but they weren't qualified to touch or take. And Mark was well aware he suffered a special kind of exclusion; something about him, some combination of appearance, manner and approach made the isolation of his life much keener than other young people's. At times he felt he was an outcast. But that would change. It was unbearable to imagine it wouldn't.

In the meantime he found ways to divert himself, ways to make the waiting time easier. There was the occasional excitement of thieving. Sometimes, the act was as fulfilling as the rewards. The only way he ever got hold of real spending money was by stealing. He stole from his mother, but that was usually a last resort; it was more common for him to steal goods from shops and sell them. Vandalism was another diversion. The excitement there was different; the destruction or mutilation of property gave Mark a powerful feeling of revenge – and of course there was the kick he got from the danger, for there was always a chance of being caught.

But the best escape he knew, the most pleasant and effective of all, was from smoking hash. He didn't much like the actual smoking of it, or the immediate effects, but what he did love were the glimpses of perfection when he was high, the glorious moments of ecstacy when it seemed that he and the world were in harmony. There was no substitute for that experience. If there was, Mark hadn't tried it yet.

At the corner of Bridge Street he stopped and thought about where he could get a fiver's worth. He didn't want to be ripped off again, so the two other dealers he knew were out. He remembered what Nick had said; he should deal with a black. There was a pub on the other side of the borough where the customers were mostly West Indians. It was a long walk, but it might be worth it.

He sighed as he turned round and began walking again. It would be so much easier if Nick would just come across and let him have some. On the other hand, he might be heading towards a new arrangement, perhaps a better one. And if he wasn't, the walk there and back would pass a bit of time.

'Did you see that?' Ali Osman said to Sue. They were standing at the door of the café. Sue had the baby with her in his pram.

'What?'

'Young Mark Fowler. He came round the corner, stopped and stared into space for a second, then turned and went off in the opposite direction.'

'He's weird, that one. I always said he was.'

'It was like he was hearin' voices,' Ali said. He turned and grinned at Sue. 'Takes all sorts, eh?' He looked down at his son, a sleeping bundle at the centre of the big pram. 'How's he been this mornin'?'

'An angel. What else do you expect?' Sue reached out and patted the child tenderly. 'It's funny, every time I bring him round to see you, he falls asleep.'

'I have that effect on a lot of people.' Ali glanced over his shoulder. 'I'll have to get back to work, love. There's people waitin'.' He kissed Sue's cheek. 'See you later, eh?'

'I'll stop by this afternoon.' She straightened the pram, aiming it towards Albert Square. 'I'm goin' back to the flat now. When Hassan's had his next feed I'll change him an' then we'll go for a walk up the public park.'

'It's a busy life, bein' a mother,' Ali said.

'Don't knock it,' Sue told him as she moved away. ''Bye, love.'

It was a busy life all right, she thought. And at times it was exhausting. But she would never have believed how gratifying it could be. She was up at all hours of the night, she spent ages washing endless bundles of nappies, there were the regular feeding

148

and bathing routines and the time absorbed in soothing and comforting the child. Sue devoted most of her day, every day, to that tiny scrap of life in the pram. By evening she was weary and drained of energy, but she couldn't remember when she had ever been so happy.

As she rounded the end of the garden in the middle of the square then crossed the road towards number 23, Reg Cox was coming out of the gate. He stopped when he saw her and craned his head towards the pram.

'Makes a lot of noise for somethin' so small,' he grunted.

Sue glared at the scruffy old man. 'I'm sorry if he disturbs you in the night,' she said stiffly. 'Cryin's his only way of lettin' me know he wants attention.'

'Oh, I wasn't complainin'.' Something like a smile cracked Reg's face, exposing discoloured teeth. 'A kiddie's got to exercise his lungs.' He nodded once, sharply, then walked away.

That had to be some kind of record, Sue thought as she parked the pram by the front door and lifted the baby out. Reg Cox had actually said something pleasant. It had never been heard of.

Hassan began to wake up as she carried him into the living room. Sue sat down, nestling him carefully against her, watching the tiny features unclench from sleep.

'You're the best baby in the world,' she said, smiling at him. 'You even softened old Reg Cox's heart.'

Feeling him move softly against her, she wondered if Hassan would go on being a miracle for her. Her entire life had been transformed by him – no one could ever know how huge the changes were. From the alternating fear and dejection of the weeks leading up to his birth, she had come to a state of contentment that was entirely new in her experience. Far from being harder than before, life was actually much easier. Even though every hour was taken up by the child in one way or another, Sue's zest for her existence made her capable and ready to take on any new pressures.

She looked round the room, reflecting how her attitude to this place had altered. From the gloom-laden certainties she'd had before they moved in, she had shifted to an attitude of bright optimism. The place was definitely pokey, there was damp in the walls, it was too dark and the bathroom arrangements were unsatisfactory. She didn't delude herself about the shortcomings. But this place was a start, it was their first home and when the baby was a little older Sue had plans for making improvements.

'Just you wait,' she told Hassan softly. 'You'll have nice bright walls around you an' a lovely soft carpet to crawl on.'

She stood up and went to the window. There was sunlight in the square; over on Bridge Street the market traders were doing steady business as people came and went, following the random routes of their individual lives. The whole scene gave Sue a warm sense of security. This was where she lived with her husband and son. They were part of something vibrantly alive, a solid community where the harshness of life was softened by mutual caring. She felt a shiver of pleasure as some children ran past. One day, her Hassan would be one of those tousle-headed rascals out on the street. She raised him gently in her arms and kissed him.

'You're my precious lad,' she whispered. 'You're my miracle.'

Over by the corner door of The Vic, Angie Watts paused on her way in. She waved across to Sue and saw her wave back. Angie hadn't seen such a change in anyone as there was in that girl. That was what becoming a mother did for you, she supposed. She elbowed her way in through the door and hoisted her bag of shopping on to the bar.

'There you go, Den. Put that lot at the bottom of the stairs for me, will you?'

'Certainly, madam.' Den took the bag through to the back. 'Will there be anythin' else?' he asked as he came to the bar again.

'Yeah.' Angie was unbuttoning her coat and nodding to a couple of regulars. 'I'll have a tonic water, I think.'

Den frowned at her. 'I thought you were goin' to take over. I've got to get down to the cash an' carry yet, an' I promised I'd get the Rover in for its service by half-twelve.'

'Just one tonic an' a sit down for five minutes,' Angie said. 'That's all I'm askin'.'

'Five minutes, then. Not a second longer.' Den jerked the cap off a tonic bottle and poured it. 'Here. Enjoy.'

Angie got on to a stool and took a sip from the glass. She didn't happen to believe that Den was going to the cash and carry, or that he was going to get a while-you-wait service done on the car, either.

But this was one of the days when she didn't really mind the deception. Her jealousy was a cyclic emotion. All she cared about, for the moment, was getting a holiday organized.

She unrolled the travel brochure she had been carrying under her arm. They had the chance of a relief manager in early September and she really fancied a break somewhere warm. The travel agent had recommended the Greek Islands, or somewhere in the Canaries. Whichever she chose, Den would put up a fight, but this time she was determined. A holiday would make all the difference to her. She stared at a picture of a golden, sun-swept beach and began to dream.

'Hello, Ange.'

She looked up. It was Lofty. He looked terrible. 'What's the matter?' she asked. 'You look like you've seen a busload of ghosts.'

'I've had one of me attacks.' He sat on the stool next to her as Den came across. 'Can I have a brandy, please?'

Angie frowned at him. So did Den.

'I really think I need one.'

Den shrugged and turned to the optic with a glass. Angie was staring at Lofty's pale, almost grey lips and the dark loops around his eyes. When he brought the money from his pocket she noticed his hand was trembling. 'What brought it on, then?'

'Oh, it's a long story.'

Den put the drink in front of him and murmured that it was on the house. 'But I won't be making a habit of this,' he warned.

'Don't worry, Den. I don't think I'll be makin' a habit of drinkin'.'

'So tell me,' Angie said. 'What was it?'

'I went for that interview I was tellin' you about.'

Angie nodded. 'The one you haven't stopped talkin' about for a week.'

'Yeah.' Lofty took a swallow of the brandy and gasped softly. 'God, that's strong.'

'Well considerin' a half of shandy practically puts you on your back, I'm not surprised the old three-star hits you with a bang. Take it easy. An' tell me what happened.' Angie's concern was to the fore again. Sometimes she felt Lofty was too vulnerable to be let out on his own. 'What kind of job was it?'

'They're a fertilizer company.'

'I thought you said it was somethin' to do with chemical manufacturin' an' that kind of thing? I expected you'd at least be makin' birth pills.'

'The job they offered me was in a big shed, well away from the rest of the place.' He shuddered on the second sip of brandy. 'I'm not surprised they kept it separate. God.' He turned to Angie, trying to express the horror of the place with twitchy little movements of his face and hands. 'It was like somethin' out of a video nasty. All dark an' shadowy, with powdery stuff clingin' to the rafters an' the walls. An' the smell. It was unbelievable.'

'What – from the fertilizer, you mean?'

'From one ingredient. The one they process in that shed. Fish meal.'

'Hell's bells. An' that's what brought on your asthma, was it?'

He nodded, then shrugged. 'Well – yes, that was

153

part of it. I was chokin' in there, tryin' to listen while this little guy told me how many bags of the fish meal had to be put in the drums for mixin' with other stuff. He was goin' on like I'd already said I'd take the job. When I finally managed to say I didn't think I could last five minutes in there, he really started lettin' me have it.'

Angie patted his arm. 'Poor Loft. They're always pickin' on you, ain't they?'

'It was his attitude. He more or less said I'd got him in the shed to waste his time. I couldn't tell him it was the Job Centre that had done it. I mean, if they'd mentioned about the fish meal, or the fertilizers . . .' He sighed. 'I can't work around any heavy quantities of powders or anythin' else that gets carried on the air. I was warned about that when me asthma first came to light. I'd have said no thanks if they'd warned me. But there he was, this little bloke, really chewin' me off as if it was my fault. I started gettin' upset an' then I had the attack. He had to help me outside. Good job I'd me inhaler with me.'

Angie watched him take another drink. His colour was coming back slowly, but he still looked pathetic and unwell. 'You need proper lookin' after, Lofty. With that condition, you need regular meals an' a bit of pamperin' now an' then. I mean a lot of it's emotional, isn't it? You need to be more settled an' have better livin' standards.'

'A decent job would give me them.' He looked down at his hands, the fingers listlessly twining with each other. 'I feel a bit of a fool, Ange.'

'We all do sometimes. You've no reason for it

154

today, though. None of this business has been your fault.'

'Yes, it has. I really thought I was goin' places with that PL twaddle. I conned *myself*. All it got me was a fobbin' off with a duff job that nobody in his right mind would take.' He made a small, humourless smile. 'I'm right back where I was. I never moved away, in fact. I'm still old deadbeat Lofty. Lofty the dopey git.'

'Oi,' Angie said sharply. 'Mind your mouth. That's a friend of mine you're talkin' about.'

'But it's true. Since they threw me out of the army I've been useless. The Service pushed me along in the right direction. They were givin' me a career an' I was fed an' clothed an' given a wage at the same time. I've never known anythin' like that, since.' His eyes had turned solemn. 'It's obvious, isn't it? I'm a loser. You can get by as a loser in the army. But not out in civvy street. Now nowadays.'

'You're just feelin' down because of the disappointment over the job, an' havin' the attack . . .'

'No, I'm truly fed up with *me*, Ange. I'm useless an' that's that.'

She could see he wasn't after her pity. He meant what he said. Angie reached out and took one of his hands between hers. 'I'll not have this, Lofty. Stop avoidin' my eyes an' look at me.' She waited until his eyes met hers. 'Now listen. In spite of what you think of yourself, you've got a hell of a lot goin' for you. I'm not butterin' you up, either. You know I wouldn't do that.'

He looked bewildered. 'What have I got goin' for me?'

'Your personality, for a start . . .'

'Come on, Angie. I've got about as much person-ality as a stale bun.'

'Your personality is attractive, Lofty. Your shy-ness is attractive, it's endearing. People trust you, too, because you're open an' honest.' She wouldn't tell him the rest, the root truth, which was that women were strongly drawn to a certain kind of vulnerability in a man – the kind that Lofty had. 'You're kind, considerate, courteous – '

'An' totally lackin' in talent or drive.'

'We can't all be tycoons, Lofty. Bein' pushy wouldn't suit you. That'd be a disaster if you ever tried it.'

He nodded. 'I found that out.'

Angie squeezed his hand tightly. 'If you want the secret of success, I'll give it to you, free of charge. Be just who you are, an' never, ever, kid yourself. It's foolin' yourself that causes more calamities than anythin'. Tryin' to fool other folk causes just about as many. You just bide your time, Lofty, an' stay unspoilt. Your chance'll come.'

When she released his hand he looked at it for a moment, as if he had been given something.

'Just one other thing, if it's any consolation. . . .' Angie got off her stool, realizing Den was about to tell her he had to go. She put her mouth close to Lofty's ear and spoke quietly. 'I know when you're workin' here I'm forever gettin' me knickers in a knot, bollockin' you for this an' that an' the other – but deep down where it matters, I like you a lot. Plenty of people do. You're one of the nice guys, Lofty.'

He watched her as she went behind the bar. If anyone had told him he could begin to feel that good on a black day like this, he wouldn't have believed them. He closed his eyes for a second, seeing the picture she'd painted of him. It wasn't much different from the picture he already had. But to know that this character – shambling and fumbling, gangling and awkward, shy and uncertain – was not necessarily repellent, was in fact *attractive* to some people, including Angie – well, that was some revelation.

'Cheers, Ange,' he said as she passed on the other side of the bar. Feeling his depression ebb swiftly away, he picked up his glass and took a gulp. A coughing fit erupted as the brandy hit his throat. It was so explosive that a man came running from the other end of the bar to slap his back.

Angie rolled her eyes and grinned at Den. 'Good old Lofty,' she murmured, watching him spluttering and gasping. 'The place just wouldn't be the same without him, would it?'

Two days before he was due to appear in court, Pete Beale sat in the living room of his mother's house with Arthur Fowler and Pauline. He had come to tell Lou that the stall would cease trading on Saturday of that week. Since he had first told her he intended to close down she had hardly spoken to him, and she refused to discuss the closure at all. Nevertheless, he felt he had to tell her when, precisely, the old family firm would cease to exist.

'She's not been in since dinner time,' Pauline told Pete as she brought him a cup of tea.

'Off gallavantin' somewhere,' Arthur added. 'Her an' Ethel. I think they were plannin' to take a walk round the park in the sun, then go to afternoon bingo.' He sighed. 'It's a full life for some folk.'

'Well, I'll come across an' see her tonight.'

'She's not goin' to like it,' Pauline said. 'She looks on that stall as a monument to our Dad, an' a few other things besides.'

'She'll have to accept it, Sis, whether she likes it or not. We're finished an' that's that.' In the past weeks Pete had lost weight. He had also been losing more of his self-confidence. He stared gaunt-eyed from Arthur to Pauline, trying to elicit a measure of sympathy. 'I would never have done this if I'd had any alternative, you both know that.'

'Of course we do,' Arthur assured him. 'Mind you, if you'd accepted my offer . . .'

'Look, Arthur, your redundancy money's all the cash you've got in the world. You'd have been throwin' good money after bad if you'd given it to me.'

'It was a loan we talked about,' Pauline reminded her brother. 'Only a loan.'

'Which you'd have had no chance of ever gettin' back.' Pete put down his cup and stood up. Lately he was too agitated to relax for long. 'How's things with you two, anyway? All I seem to talk to you about's me own heartaches.'

'Things are just the way they've been for months,' Pauline said. 'No change. No prospect of it.'

'But I keep hopin',' Arthur put in quickly. 'The one thing you can't do without is hope.'

'I think mine went down the pan somewhere along the line,' Pete said. 'What about the kids?'

Pauline shrugged. 'We hardly see them. Michelle's always over the road with Sharon. Mark – well, who knows where he goes or what he does.'

'No more of that drug business?'

Pauline shook her head.

'It's hard to tell,' Arthur said. 'He's a fly one. An' he's a loner, too. You can't find out much about a fly loner. But I just keep hopin' in that direction. It's all hope, hope, hope.'

'I'm sure he's chucked it,' Pauline insisted. 'Dr Legg's had a word with him, that was bound to have helped.'

Arthur was about to offer a cautious rebuttal when there was a knock at the front door. Pauline went to answer it. She came back after a few seconds. She looked troubled.

'It's somebody for you, Pete. He wouldn't come in. Just said he was told you were here an' he wants a word.'

'Anybody you know?' Pete asked her.

'No. Looks like some kind of official, though.'

Pete groaned. 'More trouble, I shouldn't doubt. Right, I'll see what he wants.' He nodded at his half-full cup on the table. 'Thanks for the tea.'

When he got to the front door he found Max McGinley waiting for him. Even in the heat he was wearing a dark business suit and tie.

'Am I disturbing anything?' he asked Pete.

'No, I was just leavin'.'

'In that case, perhaps you'd have time for a drink.'

159

There was no apparent warmth in the offer. He could have been asking the price of a cabbage.

'Yeah, well . . .'

'Fine. Let's go then, shall we?' McGinley turned smartly on his heel and headed towards The Vic. Pete followed him, aware again that even the man's back carried some built-in threat. He wondered what was up now.

In the pub they took their drinks to the same table they had used the first day they met. It was a table Pete had been reluctant to use the few times he had been in The Vic since then.

'I've been looking into your affairs,' McGinley said, reminding Pete of the woman in the loan office. 'It was a rather more thorough investigation than I usually need to undertake, but I believed it was necessary.'

Pete nodded, steeling himself for some new and terrible revelation about himself.

'I discovered some amazing things.' McGinley sipped his beer, frowning thoughtfully. 'I mean in this day and age, the barbarity of some people reeks of the old East End of the twenties and thirties.' He smiled faintly. 'You've had a bad enemy for a lot of years – I mean Mr Harris, of course.'

Pete nodded. 'He hates my guts.'

'But for a while he's been something of a sleeping tiger. Until it came to the siting of that vegetable shop round the corner.'

'Was he responsible for that?'

'Oh yes,' McGinley said. 'Personally responsible. As a matter of fact, other members of the consortium favoured a bigger place on the High Street. It would have been a more profitable move for them. But Geoffrey Harris has more weight than the others, so he was able to pull the rug from under your business quite easily.'

Once or twice Pete had thought of going to see Harris, after he had learned it was his former brother-in-law who had raised the firmest objection to him joining the consortium. He had resisted the impulse each time, however, when he realized how much pleasure it would have given Harris to hear him plead. If Pete had known the same man deliberately ruined him, he would certainly have gone to see him, but only to punch him in the teeth.

'I didn't think he hated me *that* much. I mean, to take a cut in his group's profits, just to get at me . . .'

'Oh, he hates you worse than you ever imagined.' McGinley's eyes read Pete's face in their disturbing way, as if he were trying to see just what could make one man loathe another so badly. 'He's very close to his sister, I suppose. He feels you took some good years away from her.'

'Not half as many as she did me out of,' Pete grunted. 'Tell me – what have you been diggin' all this up for, anyway?'

'To get my case together,' McGinley said.

'Your case? For them wholesalers, you mean?'

'No, Mr Beale. For you.' There was the fleeting trace of a smile. 'I was acting on your behalf. I grant you I should have waited to be asked, but then I didn't think you'd ever ask me.'

'Hang on.' Pete was confused. 'You're sayin' you did all this snoopin' for *me*? But why?'

McGinley made a small movement of the shoulders which, for him, did service as a shrug. 'Call it a random act of generosity. To be frank, I smelt a large and very powerful rat in the Harris connection, as soon as you mentioned it to me. So I put out the feelers, called in a favour or two and finally put together the whole picture.'

'So where does that take us?'

'Sit back and listen.' McGinley swallowed some more beer. Today, Pete had noticed, his face didn't reveal so much indifference. There was even something faintly cordial in the way McGinley sat at an angle to him, instead of setting up the square confrontation he usually preferred. 'Geoffrey Harris,' he said, 'is the man who had your van wrecked and your stock ruined.'

'What?' It was a shock, like something tangible being wedged between Pete's ribs, catching his breath. 'Are you sure?'

'Positive.'

'Jesus . . .' Pete had thought of so many possibilities, a lot of them very wild, yet he had never believed that the snooty, self-made Mr Harris would ever stoop to anything like that, no matter how much he hated him. 'Why did he do it? Because I was tryin' to get back on me feet?'

McGinley nodded. 'That's precisely why. He knows you're tenacious, so he had to pull the heart right out of you. When he learned you were trying a van round, he took immediate steps.'

'The bastard.' Pete narrowed his eyes. 'Can we definitely prove this?'

'Yes, we can. Why?'

162

'Well it's obvious, isn't it? I'll have the law down on him quicker than shit through a chicken.'

McGinley shook his head. 'No, I don't think you want to do that.'

'You're kiddin'! I'm not goin' to let that bugger get away with what he did!'

'Lower your voice, Mr Beale. People are looking.'

Pete glared across at the bar. Four heads instantly turned away. 'So what am I expected to do,' he hissed, 'after you've gone to all the trouble of gettin' proof?'

'I asked you to listen,' McGinley said. 'So do that.' He took a fat, official-looking envelope from his pocket and set it on the table. 'I set out to represent your best interests, as I do for all my clients. Getting Mr Harris banged up in jail wouldn't have been the best I could do for you. That would have been very second best. So.' He tapped the envelope. 'I got you compensation.'

Pete stared at the envelope. 'How do you mean?'

'There's three thousand pounds in there, less my modest commission. The money is yours.'

Now Pete was transfixed by the envelope.

'Take it. It won't bite.'

'But . . .' Pete's mind was spinning. The puzzlement, the too-rapid cancellation of worry, the very *presence* of so much money was overwhelming. He looked up at McGinley. 'How the hell did you manage it?'

'By offering Harris the options. He could either face the law, or pay you off. Mind you, I have to admit he was tough, at first. It was only when he'd had a few days to sleep on the prospects of life in prison, plus the terrible publicity and the loss of social standing that he'd taken years to build up – it was only then, knowing my reputation for following through, that he agreed to a settlement.'

Pete was feeling a little faint. He picked up his glass with a shaking hand and swallowed some beer. 'I can hardly believe it.'

'Believe it. You're off the hook.'

Pete was staring at the envelope again. He still hadn't touched it. 'He's a bloody mug, isn't he? I mean, he could still get handed over to the law.'

'Not by me, Mr Beale. He has my word on that. I don't break my word. He's been assured that your word, which I gave on your behalf, is just as unbreakable.'

Pete saw the warning in the renewed hardness of McGinley's eyes. He nodded. 'Fair enough.'

'You've enough there to soothe your outrage.' McGinley picked up his glass and drained it. 'Of course,' he said, putting it down again, 'the money only solves the short-term problems.'

Pete nodded. 'I'll still have to find meself another way of makin' a livin'. But this gives me time – '

'Time to wait for your customers to start coming back,' McGinley said.

Pete blinked at him.

'You see, compensation has to be just that – it has to compensate. Now I felt that the savagery of Mr Harris's action against you required more than a few thousand pounds to cancel. So the shop round the corner is going to close down. That's part of the deal.'

'Bloody hell.' Pete stared with open admiration. 'That must have taken a bit of swingin'.'

'Not really. They can move to the High Street premises, they're still vacant. Harris admitted the other members of the consortium would welcome the move.'

At last Pete touched the envelope. He patted it gingerly, as if it might vanish if he handled it too roughly. 'It's the best thing that's ever happened to me,' he said huskily. 'I get all this, I get back on me feet, an' I can keep runnin' the business.' He looked at McGinley again. 'An' to think I once thought you were the enemy.'

'Well I was, once,' McGinley pointed out.

'I'll never be able to repay you.'

'Oh, you have, believe me. I didn't give any discount on my fee.' McGinley stood up. 'I must go.' As Pete stood up he extended his hand. 'If we can do business again, let me know.'

When they got outside Pete followed McGinley to where his car was parked. 'I want to thank you again,' he said awkwardly. 'I still don't see why you did all this for me.'

'Yours was a just cause, Mr Beale. And I enjoyed playing detective against a real criminal. Most people I go out against are just businessmen who've suffered some misfortune. Besides . . .' He smiled as he took the car keys from his pocket. 'I can never resist a case where my percentage is tax free.'

September

An early mist obscured one end of the square from the other as Lou Beale, after a half-sleepless night, emerged from her front door and stood by the gate. There were the usual sounds from the Bridge Street market as traders set up their stalls. That was a reliable noise, regular as church bells, which Lou had been hearing for so long she scarcely noticed it. But this morning there was another set of sounds, clanking and discordant. They came from the misted end of the square beyond The Vic. Curious, Lou turned up her coat collar and walked towards the source of the racket.

A battered van was standing outside the boarded-up house at number 3. The noise was coming from the basement. Lou stepped close to the railings and peered down. She could hear sheet metal, planks and something boomingly hollow being moved around.

'What do you reckon it is, Lou? Vandals?'

She turned and saw Dr Legg. His question obviously wasn't serious, because he was smiling.

'There hasn't been anybody near this place in years, Doctor.'

'Since 1970, to be precise,' Legg said. 'Old Mrs Turpin was my neighbour for twenty-three years, until she passed away.'

'You don't think they're goin' to pull the house

down, do you? The square wouldn't look the same without it.' Lou had taken a long time to get used to the open end of the square where the bomb exploded and took away a building during the war. She was about to remark on that, then stopped herself. The same bomb had killed Dr Legg's wife. 'Seems they're demolishin' most of the old houses in Walford, these days.'

'It's been sold, Lou.'

'Sold? Who to?'

'A Mr Carpenter. I met him briefly the other day when he was taking a look round.'

Lou stared up at the scarred front of the house with its rotting window frames and crumbling brickwork. 'Not much of a home for anybody,' she murmured.

'He's a builder, among other things. I gather he intends to convert the basement for himself to live in. Then he'll turn the rest into flats for letting.'

Ethel Skinner had wandered up, unnoticed. She was taking Willie for his morning walk. 'Change,' she said, mildly startling Lou. 'I said so a while back, didn't I? There's big changes goin' on all round.'

'Well, we shouldn't try to stop progress,' Dr Legg said. 'We only have to keep an eye on it and control it.' He tightened his grip on his attaché case. 'Excuse me, ladies. It'll soon be surgery time.'

As he walked away the two old women stood peering into the basement area, listening to the noise. Every few seconds small pale clouds of dust emerged from the half-open door.

'What're you doin' out at this time of mornin', anyway?' Ethel asked.

'Oh, I was a bit restless, an' Pauline was goin' on at the kids, so what with the upheaval an' all I thought I'd come out an' get a bit of peace.' She had come out of the house because, towards dawn, the tightness in her chest had been making her breathless. She had put up with it as long as she could, then decided to dress and go out. When her chest was troubling her she always felt calmer and safer out of doors. 'Look Ethel,' she muttered as the basement door swung wide. 'Somebody's comin' out.'

They stared as the overall-clad figure emerged, brushing dust from his sleeves. He was tall and muscular, a handsome man in his early forties with a beret perched squarely, rather comically, on his head. It was neither his good looks nor his funny hat that drew Ethel's immediate attention, however. She nudged Lou.

'Look. He's a darkie.'

'I can see that.'

'They're movin' in all over,' Ethel said, making it sound ominous.

'He's most likely just a workman the new owner's hired.'

The man looked up and smiled broadly at them. 'Good morning, ladies,' he called. He had a rich, booming Jamaican accent. 'I'm just making a start here, clearing out my basement.' Getting no response beyond the women's cautious staring, he made a tiny bow and introduced himself. 'Carpenter's my name. Tony Carpenter. I'll be coming to live here soon.' The women glanced at each other as he stood in the doorway sniffing the air. 'A bit foggy, isn't it? But I think it'll turn out nice.'

Lou and Ethel made little unformed sounds in reply, then turned in unison and began walking towards Bridge Street.

'That's that, then,' Ethel muttered. 'He's movin' in. That's two lots we've got in the square now.' She nodded towards the flat on the corner, adjacent to the pub. It was occupied by the couple who ran the Asian Food Store on Bridge Street.

'Well, if he's as quiet as them two, he'll be no trouble.' The Asians, both in their fifties, were polite, withdrawn people. The woman never appeared to be in particularly good health. 'Best to take folk as you find them, Et.'

'I daresay.' Ethel was openly wary of coloured people. In her young days the East End's only foreigners, in any numbers, had been the Jews. She'd always known where she stood with them. Nowadays, Dr Legg was the only Jew in the district, so far as she knew. She had no idea where she stood wtih the newcomers. 'All this change,' she sighed. 'We could do without a lot of it. England soon won't be England any more.'

They turned the corner by The Vic. Ethel indicated that she would carry on walking the dog while Lou stopped to have a word with Pete and Kathy.

'What brings you out this early?' Kathy asked her.

Lou sought an excuse. The one she'd given Ethel wouldn't work with these two. 'I fancied takin' a look at the mornin'.'

That was certainly true, in part. Lou had memories of standing on that very spot, at that hour, with her young children around her as she set out the stall. It had always been a special time of day, the air cool and night-washed, carrying the odours from freshly unpacked produce along the row of barrows. It was the time of beginning, the clean start to the day when all manner of things were still to happen.

'While you're at it,' Pete said. 'You'd better take a long last look at the barrow.' He rearranged a small hill of pears, making it more symmetrical. 'I'm havin' it painted tonight. You won't know it by tomorrow.'

Lou nodded approvingly. 'As long as you keep the colour the same.'

'Don't worry,' Kathy said. 'He's a stickler for tradition.'

Lou watched Pete as he reached across the planking, shifting boxes into line and propping the cardboard labels on top. The change in him was remarkable. From the greying, faded figure of despair he'd been a couple of months ago, he'd been transformed into a youthful, energetic trader at the helm of a newly-thriving business. Lou would have liked to know more about how that had happened. Pete had been too vague. All he would tell any of them was that a friend had found out who wrecked the van, and had extracted compensation. She didn't doubt that was true, but there had to be more to it. Maybe one day he would tell her.

Lou looked up. The sun was piercing the mist, putting the soft yellow glow across the rooftops. 'It's goin' to be a nice day,' she said.

Kathy nodded. 'It's my favourite time of year, this.'

'And mine, love.'

Lou turned to face the square again. Memories rushed by, bright-lit recollections of times she had sat in that little garden, playing with the children and wondering about her Albert, off somewhere in the war. There had been times when she had wept in there, and when peace came she had held her twins close to her and watched as people danced around the trees and benches, her Albert among them.

'I'll just take a walk round for a bit,' she said. 'Pop in an' have a cup of tea later, Kathy, if you've the time.'

At the corner she met Arthur, shaved and fresh, ready to face another day of dwindling hope. 'I'm goin' across to the garage on Dover Lane,' he told her. 'They've been lookin' for somebody to run the carwash, so I hear.'

'Well you remember an' push yourself,' Lou said. 'Don't let them fob you off with any of that too-old nonsense.'

'Don't worry, Mum I'll give it all I've got.' He went off across the square, waving cheerily. As Lou crossed the road to the garden she offered up a bleak prayer for Arthur. She didn't quite know where the prayer was aimed. To providence, perhaps. It had seen Pete all right in the end.

She sat down on a bench and gazed along the brightening, shabby stretch of Bridge Street. She could see her son working, his wife dancing attendance as they got the stall shipshape. She waved to

Mark and Michelle, off to school, pausing in whatever new argument they were having to wave back.

Her chest felt better. The discomfort hadn't gone, but it was definitely better. Lou wondered if this tightness was the herald of what would finally take her away. She was nearly seventy, after all, so some sign or other was probably due. She hoped the pains and breathlessness were the earliest of warnings, if they were warnings at all. She wanted to be around this place for a long time yet.

'Mum. I've been lookin' for you.' Pauline came across from the house. She was frowning anxiously as she came and stood by the bench. 'You didn't tell me you were goin' out.'

'Oh, I just slipped away for five minutes. Wanted to get a whiff of the mornin'.'

'Are you warm enough? You haven't got your scarf on.'

'Don't fret, Pauline. I'm all right.'

Pauline sat down beside her mother. 'What's goin' on over there?' She pointed to the coloured man pushing planks into the van outside number 3.

He's bought the place,' Lou said. 'His name's Carpenter.'

'Ooh. Well, he'll add a bit of colour to the square, won't he?' Pauline giggled. 'I'll bet it's got Ethel worried.'

'Anythin' gets Ethel worried, if it happens close enough to her own doorstep.' Lou smiled at her daughter. 'It's nice out here at this time of day, isn't it?'

'Smashin'.' Pauline patted Lou's hand. 'You've spent a lot of mornin's sittin' here, haven't you?'

Lou nodded. There had been more mornings in this garden than she could count. Mornings when she couldn't sleep, mornings when worry or grief or simple impatience with life had made her seek the centre of her little world and sit there, taking stock.

'I've got to go an' get ready for work.' Pauline stood up. 'Don't sit there too long, will you? Go in an' have a hot cuppa. I'll leave a pot ready in the kitchen.'

Lou sat back. She watched Pauline go into the house, then let her eyes drift across the square. Taking stock was all there was to do now. Lou's days of doing things, of making things happen, were over.

She saw Ethel going back to her flat, pausing by the steps to talk to Lofty. Angie came out of The Vic and dumped two bulging plastic bags for the bin men. Pete threw her a wolf whistle. Angie tittered and disappeared again. Over at number 23 Sue's baby began to cry as Tony Carpenter heaved another pile of rubbish into his van.

Another day, Lou thought. Fresh beginnings with lots of things still to happen. Not a lot would happen for her, though. She didn't want it to. As long as she could take all this in from time to time, the bustling life of Albert Square, the buzzing unison of lives dominated by hope and endeavour, she would be satisfied.

She watched the thin cloud part to let through clear sunlight. The warmth touched her face and hair, soothing her. Inevitably, she knew, a time would come, perhaps soon, when she would no longer be able to sit in the garden and feel herself a part of this beloved place. but for the moment she was fine, she was content. Or as content as anyone decently should be.